MURDER ON MOTT STREET

Murder on Mott Street

a Catholic Worker mystery

Scott Schaeffer-Duffy

Haley's
Athol, Massachusetts

Haley's
488 South Main Street
Athol, MA 01331
haley.antique@verizon.net
978.249.9400

Cover photo by Joe Zarella: soup line at Saint Joseph's Catholic Worker, 115 Mott Street, New York City, 1939.

Photos used with permission from Phillip Runkel at The Catholic Worker Archives, Marquette University, Milwaukee, Wisconsin.

Copy edited by Ellen Woodbury.

Proof read by Richard Bruno.

International Standard Book Number: 978-0-9982735-3-2

for my grandchildren May, Frances, and Theo

May they always find wisdom in the past, joy in the present,
and hope in the future.

Contents

The Idea Made Me Laugh
an introduction

I never met the founders of the Catholic Worker movement. Peter Maurin died in 1949, nine years before I was born. Dorothy Day died in 1980, the year I graduated from the College of the Holy Cross in Worcester, Massachusetts. I learned of her from David O'Brien, historian of the Catholic Church in America. I never visited Maryhouse Catholic Worker in New York's Lower East Side, where Dorothy spent the last years of her life, until a week after she died. Later the same day, I attended her memorial service at Saint Patrick's Cathedral in New York City.

Although I never had the pleasure of knowing Dorothy personally, I have been blessed to know many people who did. Aside from their accounts of her, my predominant knowledge of Dorothy Day comes from her books and columns in *The Catholic Worker* newspaper and from published books written by others about her and the movement. I have listened to her on tape and have seen a movie, a documentary, and two plays about her. Additionally, I have more and more often reflected on her life and writing in the chaotic midst of my own experience as a Catholic Worker serving the poor and trying to promote peace in a world that values riches and military might.

My knowledge of Peter Maurin, the man Dorothy Day always said was the actual founder of the Catholic Worker movement, has been less detailed and more remote. I never met anyone who knew him. I've read only one book entirely devoted to him. I saw him portrayed by Martin Sheen in the movie *Entertaining Angels* but have tended to consider him less often than I have thought about Dorothy. This book is the result of my desire to know Dorothy's only child, the late Tamar Teresa Hennessy, whom I met in 1988. The idea for this novel came from Richard Douglas, a reader of my Catholic Worker community's newspaper, *The Catholic Radical*. He suggested I write a murder mystery set in 1942 with Tamar and Peter as the protagonists. At first, the idea made me laugh, but, as I thought about the possibilities, it grew on me.

After reading Kate Hennessy's book, *Dorothy Day: The World Will Be Saved by Beauty: An Intimate Portrait of My Grandmother*, I immersed myself in Catholic Worker history, focusing on the 1930s and early 1940s. I was very moved by the challenges of those years and the amazing responses to those challenges given by Peter, Dorothy, and other Catholic Workers. I also grew to appreciate the joys and difficulties of life for Tamar and wanted to bring her out of Dorothy's shadow.

Also, I was struck by how often in my years as a Catholic Worker I have met dedicated members of the movement who believe that demanding crises require at least nuancing, if not abandoning, the pacifism that Dorothy professed. I wanted to gain a better appreciation of how she, and anyone else for that matter, could embrace pacifism in the face of war with Germany and Japan. I know from personal experience as a peace activist in Bosnia, Israel/Palestine, Nicaragua, Iraq, Afghanistan, Northern Ireland, and Darfur, Sudan, how ferocious war can be. I've seen the cruelty human beings are capable of and the compassion they can exhibit toward their enemies. Having spent time with soldiers in war zones and sheltering them as homeless veterans, I empathize with them and believe, as Gandhi did, that violence is preferable to cowardice but that nonviolence is better than both. I have come to appreciate how extraordinarily difficult maintaining a pacifist conviction must have been for Dorothy Day in 1941 after the Japanese attack on Pearl Harbor and in 1945 after the atomic bombings of Hiroshima and Nagasaki.

Although what follows is a work of historical fiction, as much of it as I could manage reflects actual history. Virtually every line of Dorothy's and many of Peter's are citations of their actual words. A lengthy confrontation with an angry guest comes from an incident Dorothy described to Robert Coles for his book *Dorothy Day: A Radical Devotion*. In the afterword to this novel, I have included photographs and biographies of most of the historical figures included in this story as well as a bibliography of books I used as sources. I recommend them to readers who want to know more.

I welcome comments on historical, philosophical, and theological questions posed in these pages. As I grow older, I consider them more and more often.

A Rat

Fifteen-year-old Tamar smelled a rat. As the only daughter of Dorothy Day, co-founder of the Catholic Worker movement that feeds and shelters the poorest of the poor, Tamar was very familiar with both species of the rodent. In many ways, she found it easier to cope with the tenacious animals and their disgusting tails rather than with the legions of men trying to infiltrate the movement since its founding in 1933. The Catholic Worker's devotion to pacifism, racial and economic justice, and anarchism appalled many people. By 1941, Dorothy and her philosophical inspiration, Peter Maurin, had managed to alienate Catholic supporters of Francisco Franco in Spain, segregationists in the American South, leaders who demanded a unified front in the war against Nazi Germany and Japan, Communists who viewed the Catholic Church as a mortal enemy, and everyone who argued that voting is a civic duty. Dorothy and Peter's approach was revolutionary, but grounded as it was in the Gospels, lives of the saints, and Catholic social teaching, their approach was much more difficult to repress than that of secular radicals of the 1920s swept up in government raids, jailed, and even exiled.

And so, on that bitterly cold December afternoon in 1941 less than three weeks after the US entered World War II, it would surprise no one to see stool pigeons attempting to worm their way into Saint Joseph's Catholic Worker, the five-story, double tenement at 115 Mott Street in the heart of Little Italy, New York City's most crowded slum.

Feds, reporters, and just plain disgruntled people often turned up posing as eager volunteers or the down and out. It was usually pretty easy to spot them. Their eagerness to get Catholic Workers to say something potentially traitorous or heretical gave them away. More often than not, they left of their own accord frustrated by the fact that Catholic Workers seemed more interested in Peter Maurin's goal of "constructing a society where it's easier to be good" than in overthrowing governments or any nefarious plots. The man in the threadbare overcoat and snow-covered fedora, his hands buried deep in his pockets in hope of forestalling frostbite, stood indistinguishable from the rest of the dejected souls shuffling along in the soup kitchen line. He asked no questions. He barely looked up from the ground and, with the gusto of a someone who had not eaten for a long time, slurped what was ladled out to him. He might have passed through in anonymity were it not for Tamar.

Seated on an empty vegetable crate near the doorway where she waited for her mother to come from working on the soup line, Tamar was struck by something those standing around her would miss: the man's shoes. Although only the tips of them poked out from the tattered hem of his baggy pants, she could tell they were expensive. It was not an impossible incongruity. Once in a while, high-class items showed up in clothing bins at thrift stores. Often, a man who had lost his job, family, and sobriety, not necessarily in that order, would desperately hold onto one last item from his former life. It might be a musical instrument, an article of clothing, or a book. Whatever it might be, he clung to it as a last vestige of dignity.

What set Mr. New Shoes apart was that, when Tamar raised an eyebrow, he turned slightly away, loosened his belt, and hid his shoes from view. That made her at once curious and suspicious. If she had not been so, more people would have been murdered.

Road to Mott Street

It was a circuitous and bumpy road that led Tamar to perch on a crate in a soup kitchen. She was born on March 4, 1926, in Manhattan to Dorothy Day and Forster Batterham. That she was born at all was something of a miracle. When her parents first met in 1916, Dorothy was a left-wing journalist with no religious affiliation. Dorothy's friends were hard-drinking Communists, actors, authors, and other bohemians. Tamar's less flamboyant father was a biologist and fisherman with an anarchist's suspicion of church and state. While Dorothy had an appreciation for spirituality, her closest association with the Church was her friendship with the lapsed Catholic playwright, Eugene O'Neill, as well as her journalistic forays into slums where she saw immigrants attending religious ceremonies she did not understand. Neither Dorothy nor Forster was drawn to the other at first, but after years of diverse occupations to support herself as a writer, a painful break-up with a newspaperman named Lionel Moise, and a loveless civil marriage to Berkeley Tobey that included an affluent life in Europe, Dorothy yearned for more stability and direction. Forster answered part of her yearning. In a cottage she bought with proceeds from her autobiographical novel, *The Eleventh Virgin*, Dorothy and Forster entered into a happy common-law union.

Because of complications from an abortion at the end of her relationship with Lionel, Dorothy assumed she could not have children. It came as a pleasant surprise when she got pregnant and safely delivered Tamar. The little family might have lived happily ever after if Dorothy had not gravitated ever closer to Catholicism and decided to have Tamar baptized at Our Lady Help of Christians Roman Catholic Church against Forster's will. While Dorothy and Forster loved each other passionately, their personal integrity on the matter of faith tore them apart. Not long after Dorothy herself became Catholic, the days of both parents delighting in Tamar together—watching her take her first steps on the sandy beach, say her first words, and learn to sing—came to an end.

∞

In 1930, Tamar and her mother left New York for California when Dorothy accepted a three-month contract as a script-writer for Pathé Studios. Gone was the time when Tamar could be sure she'd always have one parent or the other near at hand. From then on, she spent most of her time with other relatives, with Dorothy's friends, in sundry more-or-less reliable forms of day care, or at boarding schools.

When her contract at Pathé expired, Dorothy moved with Tamar to Mexico City where she found cheap lodging with a Mexican family. She worked as a secretary for Katherine

Anne Porter, a writer who won a National Book Award and a Pulitzer Prize in 1966. Despite Katherine's fondness for Dorothy, she shared Malcolm Crowley's assessment that Dorothy had no talent for writing.

Only after taking Lionel Moise's parting advice that she should write "personally" did Dorothy's work gain traction. An article about Tamar's birth that ran in *The New Masses* was particularly good. When she and Tamar met the artist Diego Rivera, who had seen Dorothy's article while he visited Russia, he exclaimed, "I know this little girl!" Tamar may well have answered in Spanish, a language she absorbed quickly.

Her mother marveled, as all parents do, to see her daughter discover the wonders of life. She never forgot how Tamar asked, "Does the Blessed Mother mind if I say my prayers standing on my head?" and "How can I pray when I have to keep laughing?"

Unfortunately, Tamar contracted malaria, prompting Dorothy and Tamar to return to the US for medical care paid for by Forster. When she recovered, Dorothy uprooted Tamar again, this time for her grandparents' home in Florida. Dorothy's unrest continued in Florida. Many times, Dorothy reconsidered a reunion with Forster, a fantasy that took her four full years to abandon once and for all.

Eventually, Dorothy's love of the vibrancy and needfulness of New York outweighed her resolve to give a wide birth to Forster. Once back in Manhattan, she plunged into writing about capitalism, militarism, and racism for Catholic and socialist papers, but she struggled to reconcile her new faith with her old passion for social justice. Her disquiet peaked on December 8, 1932, in Washington, DC, where she had just covered the Hunger March of thousands who demanded concrete action to alleviate the suffering of the Great Depression. As a reporter and not as a delegate at the march, Dorothy felt extremely low. She went into the crypt chapel at what would become the Basilica of the Immaculate Conception and, with anguished tears, prayed that God would show her a way to use her talents for the workers and the poor.

Upon returning to the Lower East Side, she found Peter Maurin waiting for her. The introduction of Peter Maurin into the life of her mother profoundly affected Tamar as much as did the absence of her father. A fifty-five-year-old French peasant, Maurin had come a long way from his family's farm in France to Canada and then the United States. He worked with immigrants, blacks, and many others as a ditch digger, lumberjack, miner, building contractor, railroad worker, janitor, and, finally, teacher of French. He had known privation and comfort but came to reject the latter as incompatible with his growing philosophy inspired in many ways by Saint Francis of Assisi. By the time he met Tamar's mother, Peter was an itinerant preacher and philosopher with a vision of Catholics setting the world afire by taking Christ's most challenging teachings to heart. Unlike the Communists who blamed everything on the wealthy bosses and their stooges, Peter advocated a personalist revolution that "always started with *I*, not with *they*." Peter expounded his views in pithy verses Dorothy's brother John called "Easy Essays." In one, he famously wrote:

The world would be better off
if people tried to be better.
And people would become better
if they stopped trying to be better off.

For when everybody tries to become better off,
nobody is better off.
But when everybody tries to become better,
everybody is better off.

Everybody would be rich
if nobody tried to become richer.
And nobody would be poor
if everybody tried to be poorest.

And everybody would be what we ought to be
if everybody tried to be what we want the other
 one to be!

Peter broke with many social and political conventions
of his time. While more and more Americans gravitated
to cities, he called for a green revolution to create farming
communes and thereby restore the dignity of workers crushed
by industrialization. He refused to consume anything not
grown locally, including coffee. He gave away everything he
had and depended on others to reward his labor not as a wage
but as a gift. To enhance his understanding of the plight of
black Americans, he lived for two years in Harlem, and at a
time when anti-Semitism was rampant, he appealed for the
admission of all German Jewish refugees to the United States.
At an anti-Nazi protest, Peter carried a sign that read, "Spiri-
tually, we're all Semites."

Of him, Dorothy would later write:

Peter rejoiced to see men do great things and dream
their dreams. . . . He made you feel a sense of mission as
soon as you met him. He did not begin by tearing down or
by painting so intense a picture of misery and injustice that
you burned to change the world. Instead, he aroused in you
a sense of your own capacities for work, for accomplishment.
He made you feel like you and all people had great and
generous hearts with which to love God.

Dorothy's encounter with the pious visionary inspired
her to start what she later called "the only paper in the world
published by a group of lay Catholic pacifists." Setting it up
as a religious alternative to the Communists' mouthpiece,
The Daily Worker, she called it *The Catholic Worker*. Its pages
overflowed with news of anti-Semitic outrages in Hitler's
Germany, lynchings of blacks in the American South, and
violence against striking workers in more places than anyone
had imagined. Its distinctly Catholic editorials advocated for
social justice, pacifism, and personal care for the millions in
desperate need.

Peter, who preferred the name *Catholic Radical* over
Catholic Worker, advocated within its pages for going to the
roots of Catholicism to a time when Christians performed
the works of mercy themselves instead of passing off to the
state responsibility for those in need. Recalling the early and
medieval Church's eagerness to shelter the homeless, Peter
called for the creation of houses of hospitality where the poor
would be welcomed as "angels in disguise" rather than bums.
Peter's appeal for hospitality took the words off the printed
page and created a movement. Although Dorothy waded into

picket lines, slums, and sweatshops to get authentic stories for *The Call* and other socialist papers, she could always hold the poor at arm's length. Her writing for *The Catholic Worker*, on the other hand, drew the destitute to the Day-Maurin front door pleading for food and shelter. Even as the numbers of needy at their doorstep grew, a cup of coffee and bowl of soup weren't too difficult to manage.

Finding room for them to sleep, on the other hand, proved another matter altogether. The office was tiny. After a homeless woman, whom Dorothy turned away, threw herself in front of a train, the suicide shamed Dorothy into scraping together funds to rent space where they could offer hospitality. She christened the small apartment on Charles Street Saint Joseph House, a Catholic Worker community that would later move to Mott Street and then to East First Street.

To Dorothy and Peter's surprise, in little more than a year, *The Catholic Worker* grew from its first printing of 2,500 copies to more than 100,000. It would peak at 150,000. Catholic Worker houses of hospitality and Catholic Worker farms, another of Peter's ideas, opened across the United States. The astonishing growth demanded a great deal from Dorothy, and, by association, from Tamar. Speaking engagements around the country (something Dorothy always dreaded), attending daily Mass, answering mail, resolving conflicts, and keeping up with voluminous amounts of reading curtailed Dorothy's one-on-one time with Tamar. So often was Tamar in the company and care of other adults that she called her mother Dorothy like everyone else did. For hours at a time, Tamar sat in the corner of smoke-filled rooms listening to adults talk about all manner of heady things. Given how much time she spent in the company of intellectual adults, it's not surprising how mature Tamar was. Yet she still found joy in activities suited to her age. Together with two young Catholic Worker volunteers, Joe Zarella and Gerry Griffin, she formed The Hot Chocolate and Walking Club. The group went on expeditions to museums and parks, topping the outings off with cocoa at the Automat, a unique and popular cafeteria. For several years, Tamar also boarded on weekdays at The Academy of Saint Dorothy, a Catholic school on Staten Island, in part through contributions from Forster. Although the shortage of personal time with her daughter always troubled Dorothy, Tamar coped remarkably well. Once while attending to a visitor, Dorothy forgot Tamar in the tub. When Dorothy returned, she was pleasantly surprised to find Tamar happily making boats out of soap. Tamar paid no mind to the fact that the water had long since grown cold.

While it may not always have been true, Dorothy was generally right in saying, "Tamar enjoyed the freedom my preoccupations gave her." Such freedom from parental oversight would prove providential.

Becoming a Sleuth

Besides boredom, another reason prompted Tamar to scrutinize the man in the new shoes. Her mother had come to believe it was a Christian duty to see Jesus in the downtrodden, but Tamar had witnessed a number of harrowing instances when drunk or mentally unstable men had threatened to harm and even kill others at Saint Joseph's. While Dorothy looked deep into a person to discover goodness, Tamar was more wary and likely to be on alert for hidden danger. Rooted as it was in Dostoevsky's "harsh and dreadful love," Dorothy's faith had taken many decades of hard experience and prayer to acquire. It was not something that could be passed down to a child as a *fait accompli*.

Added to the difference in outlook, on that particular day, Dorothy had just returned from speaking at Saint Finbar's in Brooklyn and Saint Patrick's in Elmira and from visiting the Baltimore Catholic Worker and friends in Montreal. She had been up late the night before writing her column for the January, 1942, newspaper.

As a pacifist, Dorothy's task was not easy. American antiwar sentiment swelled in 1919 after 320,000 US soldiers were killed or wounded in what was billed as "the war to end all wars." Although antiwar feeling diminished over time, it remained strong enough to keep the US on the sidelines while much of Asia fell to the Japanese, Spain fell to fascists, and Poland, Denmark, Belgium, Luxemburg, Netherlands, France, Yugoslavia, Greece, and a third of the Soviet Union fell to the Nazis. Everything changed on the morning of December 7, 1941 when a Japanese surprise attack on Pearl Harbor, Hawaii, left 3,576 Americans dead or wounded. In less than twenty-four hours, the US declared war on Japan, and three days later on Germany and its ally Italy. Despite virtually unanimous American enthusiasm for war, Dorothy proclaimed, "We continue our pacifist stand." With the bodies of American sailors in Hawaii not yet returned to their families for burial, Dorothy's editorial was nothing less than stunning. Considering how much it cost *The Catholic Worker* in lost subscriptions, donors, and closed houses of hospitality, the editorial was a remarkable act of integrity and faith. With clarity seldom seen in the early days of war fever, Dorothy wrote,

> We are still pacifists. Our manifesto is the Sermon on the Mount, which means we will try to be peacemakers. Speaking for many of our conscientious objectors, we will not participate in armed warfare or in making munitions, or by buying government bonds to prosecute the war, or in urging others to these efforts.

And yet, as one at once very Catholic *and* genuinely American, she went on to say,

But neither will we be carping in our criticism. We love our country and we love our president. We have been the only country in the world where men of all nations have taken refuge from oppression. We recognize that while in the order of intention we have tried to stand for peace, for love of our brother, in the order of execution we have failed as Americans in living up to our principles. . . .

With the future of the young Catholic Worker movement on her shoulders, it's small wonder that Dorothy did not latch onto Tamar's expressed desire to ferret out the true purpose of Saint Joseph House's latest wolf in sheep's clothing.

"New shoes?" her mystified mother asked before saying, "I don't know, Tamar. While it's good to be curious, we must all keep custody of the eyes. After all, we'll never see things spiritual if we are distracted by the minutiae of the physical."

Annoyed that her news had been met with a kind of religious "run-along-dear" dismissal, Tamar wandered into the crowded dining room where Peter harangued a distracted crowd about Catholicism, personalism, distributism, decentrism, and other isms. As Tamar approached and Peter's words sailed over the heads of his targets, a spot opened up by an Ade Bethune mural of the jailed Saint Peter being visited by an angel. Sidling close to Peter, the elderly man many believed to be a prophet, albeit one who hardly ever let others get a word in, Tamar continued to wonder about the man in the new shoes. She could just make him out in the opposite corner where he slouched in seeming exhaustion. After a furtive glance in her direction, he gathered his coat around his broad shoulders, turned the collar up, pulled his hat down over this brow, and made a hasty departure. Convinced that her scrutiny had prompted him to flee, Tamar wondered if he would not return in a more convincing disguise.

Meanwhile, the last of Peter's targets had slipped away. He took a deep breath and sighed before noticing Tamar leaning against his great coat. "*Ma petite fille*," he asked, "Are you the only one who wants to hear me speak?"

Engrossed as she was in her musings, Tamar failed to hear a word he said.

Although he had a reputation for relentless proselytizing, Peter was not without sensitivity to the feelings of others. He bent down, tilted his head, lifted her chin gently, and asked, "Why is your mind so far away?"

Surprised but not displeased, Tamar told him what she had seen and why it troubled her.

Peter listened closely, rocked back and forth for a minute, and replied, "Our Savior warned us that unless we become like little children, we will never enter the Kingdom of God. Perhaps, you see what we grownups are too blind to notice."

Encouraged by the respect he showed her, Tamar asked, "So, what should we do if he comes again?"

Not put off in the slightest by her presumption that they were now partners, Peter tapped her temple twice and said, "Notre Dieu did not give us brains for nothing: we investigate."

She opened her mouth in surprise, but before she could find a single word, he continued, "As Mounier says, 'Prepare for opportunities, don't wait for opportunities to take you by surprise.' You and I will look into this, but we will not be so clumsy as Monsieur Nouvelles Chaussures. Oh, no. We will observe discreetly, first one and then the other, and confer afterwards in private."

And so the stage was set.

The Murderer

Manhattan's Lower East Side, unlike the neatly numbered streets of Midtown, edged the original Dutch settlement with streets that grew spontaneously to meet needs and avoid natural barriers. It was easy to get lost in the Lower East Side's Bowery, Chinatown, and Little Italy, and the neighborhood's danger equaled that of Hell's Kitchen, the Irish slum farther north. Tenements, brownstones, sweatshops, meat packing warehouses, diners, churches, synagogues, storefronts, fish markets, bakeries, flop houses, pawn shops, and bars jostled for purchase in narrow Lower East Side streets where sunlight seldom reached the ground. The rumble of trains in the subway below the streets mixed with the din of automobiles, buses, cabs, and trucks above ground. Malodorous air mixed with a spew of steam, soot, exhaust, and, all too often, the scent of garbage, urine, and vomit. A million people—immigrants and natives, underemployed, unemployed, and derelict—squeezed together in uneasy proximity without much sympathy or tolerance for those outside their own parochial circles. The mostly Irish police made only occasional shows of force. Corpses in out-of-the-way places more often got discovered by their stench than by other means. The environment was a haven for crime. City Hall, Police Headquarters, and the Stock Exchange had long ago claimed space not that far off, but the area around Mott Street may as well have been another planet, a world whose inhabitants had to fend for themselves.

In that no-man's land hours after he'd slipped out of Saint Joseph's, the man whose few associates knew him only as Thirteen rinsed his bloody hands in water trickling out of a nearly frozen drainpipe to create a scarlet pool of ice that quickly solidified on the cobbled-stoned street below. In one of the more decrepit nooks of the borough on such a frigid night, there were no spectators. The brief cry of his victim had aroused no one. Save the unexpectedly messy nature of the exsanguination, all had gone well. Thirteen's pulse had not quickened. His breathing was even, his visage placid, his mind already on the unfinished business ahead.

Before a sheen of ice could form on his palms, Thirteen dried them with a clean handkerchief, replaced his gloves, and walked calmly away in no particular direction. The consummate professional, the burly man of unremarkable face held himself to the highest standards. While his task was murder, he was neither a psycho nor sociopath. Those who took lives for pleasure, attention, material gain, or on a whim disgusted him. No, in both method and purpose, Thirteen soared above common butchery. He came and went like an invisible plague, a pestilence the public recognized only when the contagion spread widely and the host was long gone.

Were it not for miniscule doubt upsetting his peace of mind, he might have gone directly to his temporary lodging. He was too experienced not to realize that the girl at the soup kitchen had marked him because of the shoes he had presumed would go unseen. Such presumption was inexcusable to him, and he would be much more surreptitious in his next foray. All would be well. The oversight would be swept away by ultimate success. Why should it be any different than it had been in Chicago or Los Angeles? And yet, the look on that girl's face had been more pregnant with knowledge than he liked. She just could be the rare individual whose instincts rose above the pathetic minimum. She could be a problem to be dealt with.

But any deviations from the plan risked unintended consequences. He had been sternly warned to pursue modifications only as a very last resort. For now, he resolved to merely keep an eye out for her. Satisfied, Thirteen said to himself "Enough" before walking calmly away.

Before dawn broke, though, Thirteen sat bolt upright in bed, bathed in sweat despite having left a window open a crack. As with most nights, a singular nightmare disturbed his sleep by a scene of himself wandering through unspeakable destruction and carnage, a tableau out of a Bosch painting. Incinerated and dismembered bodies of men, women, and even children lay everywhere. The few badly burned survivors pitifully begged for water. An infant tried in vain to nurse from the corpse of her dead mother. The sky was black although it was midday. Fires raged on the horizon. Beside himself, only one other stood upright in the scene: an older man he knew all too well, a grim visionary clad in a disturbingly clean suit and tie. Before that middle-class apparition could utter a word, Thirteen knew what would come. He would be blamed for all the horror of the scene.

"You are responsible," Thirteen heard for the umpteenth time, "unless . . . ."

He wondered why he kept having the dream. It wasn't as if he needed convincing. He was a hundred percent on board with the mission. He would not be the weak link. The previous agents had done well to a point and then failed to complete the task, but he would not disappoint. He embodied the avenging angel sent by God to kill all the first-born Egyptians. His duty required obedience without question. Although he could not see it all, what he knew of the big picture eradicated doubt.

After rinsing his face in the room's sink, he dried it with a hand towel and returned to bed to try to eke out a couple more hours of sleep. Quite unexpectedly, though, he had a different dream that found him climbing a hill with the teenager from Saint Joseph's. She looked at him with affection and asked, "Where is the lamb for the burnt offering?" Deep in his breast, he felt the torment of the prophet Abraham whom God ordered to kill his only son. Again, Thirteen woke with a start, and this time an atom of uncertainty crept through his conviction to see his grisly assignment to its conclusion.

Another Sighting

The next day, Peter waylaid Tamar prior to her sojourn with her mother at the Staten Island cottage and announced, "I believe I have seen him again."

"Really?" she replied.

"In Union Square. The Communists were crowing about how Stalin stood alone against the Nazis. They see everything through a red lens. Their passion for class warfare blinds them to its personal impact. They cannot imagine a free association of workers and scholars, rich and poor. When I stood up to say that strikes don't strike me, they pushed me aside, but I am not discouraged. I will go back later."

Before he got completely sidetracked, Tamar said, "And I'm sure you will set them straight, but what of the man from last night?"

"Ah, oui, Monsieur Nouvelles Chaussures. For a long time, I did not recognize him. Unlike the quiet fellow we saw, he was dressed like a dock worker and argued loudly in a mix of Russian and English. I saw him head east on Sixteenth Street with a Wobbly." Tamar knew that "Wobbly" was the popular name for a member of the International Workers of the World or IWW, an anarchist labor union that welcomed all nationalities, races, and sexes.

"How did you know it was our man?" Tamar asked.

"His build, the slight crook in his nose, but mostly his eyes," said Peter with an animated expression. "A thief can dress like a king, but his eyes will give him away. His voice and occasional laugh seemed genuine, but his eyes, they were not. They hinted at a dark purpose. I fear that this man is more than he seems."

"Maybe he's a gangster or an FBI agent," she conjectured.

"*C'est possible.* They both hate the Wobblies." Indeed, J. Edgar Hoover, the formidable head of the Federal Bureau of Investigation, kept a close eye on left-wingers of all stripes, including Dorothy Day and all Catholic Workers. And the Teamsters Union, among others, had a reputation for coziness with organized crime.

"Keep your eyes and ears open," Peter advised, "and head down."

The Seashore

Later, while her mother listened to a performance of *La Traviata* on the radio, Tamar braved the cold to collect seashells. Love of the opera was one of her parents' shared passions that did not excite Tamar. Truth be told, she preferred listening to radio plays like *The Inner Sanctum Mysteries* or *The Adventures of the Thin Man*, but even opera was better than Roosevelt's boring *Fireside Chats*, especially when they were constantly interrupted by commentary from her mother, Peter, or sundry anarchists.

Walking on the seashore was one of Tamar's great joys. Had it not been for the opera, Dorothy would gladly have joined her. In summertime, they swam, dug for clams, and harvested mussels. All year round, they walked the beach, sometimes praying the rosary together, sometimes collecting driftwood to burn, sometimes chatting, and sometimes just taking the salty air in silence. Although Tamar and Dorothy had strolled the storied beaches of California, Mexico, and Florida, they always considered Staten Island's shore their favorite.

That's not to say Tamar didn't have fond memories of other beaches. When she was fourteen, she took the bus by herself to meet Dorothy in Atlantic City, where she and her mother planned to celebrate Thanksgiving. Dorothy had been on a month-long speaking trip that concluded in New Jersey where the Congress of Industrial Organizations (CIO) scheduled its convention. No Norman Rockwell family gathering for them. Mother-daughter time had to be squeezed between Dorothy's reporting and writing. But after noisy meetings in a boardwalk hotel, Dorothy and Tamar delighted in walking along the water, basking in warm sunlight, and comparing cries of seagulls with those of unionists. Dorothy was most impressed with John L. Lewis, a hard fighter for miners and determined opponent of war. Pointless carnage of the so-called Great War of the 'teens underscored by bloodshed of the current conflict left Dorothy no doubt about the new war's immorality. In her travels, she had met coal miners and understood their deplorable wages and sometimes deadly working conditions.

But not all Tamar's visits to the shore were truncated affairs. During their time in Florida, her mother peeled herself away from writing her umpteenth unpublished novel for a leisurely swim, walk, or time reading at the beach. Tamar once apprenticed to Ade Bethune at her workshop in Newport, Rhode Island, where diverse beaches, like chocolates in a Whitman Sampler, abounded. When not learning how to make drawings, prints, or stained-glass windows, Tamar sat by Narragansett Bay and looked towards Jamestown Island, jumped in the waves at Bailey's, swam in the sheltered water at Gooseberry, or looked down from the heights at the surf from the cliffside path that skirted the Vanderbilt mansion.

Ade, with her exotic Belgian accent and wonderful enthusiasm, made a charming host. Although Dorothy had embraced an ever more serious religiosity with the growth of the Catholic Worker, Ade insisted that Dorothy was at heart "bright, lively, witty, sarcastic, enthusiastic, energetic, and open-hearted." While making a print of Saint Teresa of Avila holding a tambourine, Ade reminded Tamar that her middle name, Teresa, was taken from the joyful Spanish saint who let her nuns dance. It was Ade who perused an early copy of *The Catholic Worker* and asked, "Where is the art?" From then on, Ade's creations, joined later by the works of Fritz Eichenberg, Rita Corbin, Brian Kavanagh, and others, greatly improved the paper. One issue included Tamar's sketch of black convicts in Florida.

Ade not only helped beautify the paper, but she also tackled the dreary inside of Saint Joseph's, a decrepit place that looked and smelled terrible. Taking a cue from Dorothy's suggestion that she depict saints at work, Ade painted a mural of Saint Francis sweeping the floor, the Virgin Mary sewing, and young Jesus doing carpentry. Tamar also liked that, since 1936, an Ade original graced the newspaper's masthead and became the emblem of the Catholic Worker movement. Not favoring the torturous visage of Christ crucified that dominated Catholicism, Ade created an image of a hale and hearty Jesus with arms around the shoulders of two workers, one of them black and the other white. A cross graced the background. Ade's iconic image would remain unchanged until 1983 when, in response to growing sensitivity about sexism, she replaced the white worker with an immigrant woman and child.

But on that gray December afternoon in 1941, despite the countless "Hail Marys" Tamar had previously recited on Staten Island, religion was far from her mind. Like her father, Tamar loved the sea just for itself. As she walked with the wind at her back, she was drawn to treasures cast ashore by the tide and waves. Before long, her pockets bulged with shiny pebbles and shells. She loved them all but had a special affinity for scallops. Their design recalled the fans used by geishas in Gilbert and Sullivan's *Mikado*, a play she had seen at a local high school.

"Why can't life be like a play?" she wondered, "Or better yet, like a movie?" When the mood struck her, Dorothy took Tamar on a spontaneous outing to a see a Shirley Temple or other frivolous film.

"Why must I be bored, frightened, shy, or lonely?" Tamar wondered. "Why can't I be brash and brave like Rosalind Russell in *His Girl Friday*? She ran circles around Cary Grant. Mr. New Shoes wouldn't stand a chance against an intrepid reporter like Hildy," an ironic compliment, considering that her own mother was about as intrepid a reporter as there ever was. "Hildy," Tamar reasoned, "wouldn't be put off by anyone. She was a tough woman in a man's world. Why shouldn't I crack this case wide open? If Peter can see through the scoundrel's disguise, so can I. My eyes will be extra peeled from now on."

As it turned out, she didn't need to peel them for very long. Almost immediately, she spied something peculiar farther down the windswept beach. When she got a few feet away, she could clearly see a young woman's body tangled in sea weed and half buried in the sand right at the edge of the surf. Although Tamar wished it were not, the ghostly pale face was upturned. Tamar didn't need a medical degree to see that someone had slit the throat of the unfortunate soul.

Thunderstruck by the corpse's grisly appearance and putrid smell, Tamar dropped the shells in her hands, fell to her knees, and vomited. After collecting herself as best as she could, Tamar ran back to tell her mother.

"Thank goodness her eyes were closed," she thought.

Shaken as she was, Tamar nonetheless felt impatient to share her discovery with Peter. Maybe there was something of Hildy in her after all.

More Killing

The teen detective had to wait until Maurin returned from a visit to the Catholic Worker farm, called Maryfarm, in Easton, Pennsylvania. And then she had to wait several hours more for her late-sleeping partner in crime-solving to attend the noon Mass at the new Saint Andrew's Church, built three years earlier on the site of the Five Points slum. A devout Catholic, Peter went to Mass every day and then stayed afterwards for an hour of meditation. Perhaps it was where he got the strength to talk so much the rest of the time.

During Peter's absence, Tamar learned more about the murder predominantly from Stanley Vishnewski, a twenty-five-year-old who intended to visit the Catholic Worker for only a day but ended up staying, for the most part, until his death in 1979. The tall, blue-eyed son of Lithuanian immigrants felt disillusioned by typical offerings of Catholic parishes, which he called The Five Bs: Bridge, Beer, Bazaars, Bowling, and Bingo. He rejected the clerical prejudice that the laity are "second-class citizens whose main function is to fall on their knees and open their purses." Stanley believed the hard teachings of the Gospel were meant for everyone.

On his first visit to Saint Joe's, Stanley noticed that the small kitchen was dominated by a round table, something that made him think of King Arthur and his knights. Talking with Peter reinforced his first impression. He resonated with Dorothy's description of *The Catholic Worker* as a newspaper:

> For those who are sitting on park benches in the warm spring sunlight.
>
> For those who are huddling in shelters trying to escape the rain.
>
> For those who are walking the street in the all but futile search for work.
>
> For those who think that there is no hope for the future, no recognition of their plight.

Stanley enthusiastically volunteered to write articles, help edit, and sell the paper for a penny a copy up and down the streets of New York. Sometimes finding support and at other times derision, he also waded into the picket lines of striking workers to talk to them about God.

That difficulty paled in comparison to the risks of getting caught up in a riot or violent police raid, something that happened to him at least seven times. In one instance, he got credit for putting himself in the way of a mounted policeman whose horse may otherwise have trampled Dorothy. A faith-filled and hard-core activist on the street, Stanley had a softer side at Saint Joseph's, where he often lightened the mood by singing or playing the ukulele. Described by Dorothy as having "a distinct style and humor, a freshness that is rare,"

Stanley always displayed kindness to and earned popularity with Tamar.

From him, she learned that the murdered woman, Veronica by name, was an aspiring poet whose verses resembled the published work of Ruth Lechlitner, author of *A Winter's Tale*. Everyone expected Veronica's work to appear eventually in *Poetry* magazine as Lechlitner's had, an expectation that would never come to fruition because of the murder. Veronica, like Dorothy in her early years, received rejection after rejection. She more often looked for pennies from heaven than for paychecks for her craft.

"If robbery was the motive," Tamar mused, "the thief couldn't have gotten much. But then again, maybe Veronica's poverty frustrated the robber enough to murder her, although that seems unlikely given the manner of her demise."

While Tamar had no direct experience of robbery, she imagined that a thief would display his weapon to frighten a person into giving up his or her wallet. He wouldn't slit a woman's throat from behind. The coroner's report also ruled out sexual assault and signs of a struggle. Veronica's murder was swift, disconcerting, and incomprehensible. It posed, also, a much bigger mystery to spring on Peter than the now almost forgotten case of Mr. New Shoes.

And so Tamar conquered her typical shyness around adults and approached Peter confidently. Peter sat reading a newspaper as he often did when not preaching theology and philosophy.

Overcoming concern that it would be rude to interrupt him, she clasped her hands behind her straightened back, cleared her throat, and announced, "Peter, I have news."

To her surprise, he lowered the paper and stared as if she were not there. Clearly, something he had just read had shaken him.

Not to be deterred, Tamar repeated somewhat less confidently, "Peter, I have news."

All at once, as if she had just appeared, he greeted her distractedly, "Oh, *bonjour*, Tamar."

"Well," she replied, "do you want to hear my news or not?"

Setting the paper aside, he nodded, "*Certainement*. Of course. My ears are yours."

Her enthusiasm restored, she detailed how she had discovered Veronica's body and gave him the subsequent news that told much and nothing simultaneously.

While Tamar expected Peter to be shocked, she was unprepared for the horror that spread across his face during her narrative.

"Did you know her?" she asked.

"No," he answered as he sank back into his chair.

"Then, what are you thinking?"

He removed his glasses, wiped them with a handkerchief, and let out a deep breath before saying, "It seems we have stumbled onto a puzzle far beyond the cost of a pair of shoes."

"Yes, indeed," she said. "This new mystery dwarfs the old."

"But there you are mistaken . . . ," he said before announcing, "The two are one."

Before she could ask, "What in the world do you mean?" he gathered up the newspaper, opened it to the intended page, and presented it. At first, nothing caught her attention, but then she saw what disturbed Peter. In the bottom right hand corner appeared an article entitled, "Murder in Manhattan." It sensationally mused that a young man named Fitzpatrick may have been killed by a Jack the Ripper copycat. She saw exactly what Peter meant when she read that the victim's throat had been cut from ear to ear and that his body was found in Gramercy Park, three blocks northeast of Union Square.

After a minute's silence, she whispered, "Do you think it could have been the man you saw with Mr. New Shoes?"

"I do not know. I am not sure of the Wobbly's name," he admitted. "But I fear it could be."

With the revelation, Tamar felt the need to sit down next to Peter. Neither said a word for a long time until Tamar concluded, "I suppose this means our sleuthing is over."

Peter furrowed his brow and replied in a measured voice, "Not necessarily. If we are right, there is danger. Véronique's murder proves that. But you and I, we are personalists. As Mounier said, 'Personal man is not desolate, he is a man surrounded, on the move, under summons.' When we hear that summons, we must act."

Taken aback, Tamar asked, "But how?"

"With wisdom, caution, and . . . ," he replied with a raised finger, " . . . stealth."

"That sounds easy in theory but, like my mother says, in reality it could be 'harsh and dreadful.'"

"Indeed. We must seek guidance."

"From where? No one will listen to me and, meaning no disrespect, Peter, you have a hard time keeping an audience, too."

Without taking offense, he said, "We must pray for wisdom. The Bible tells us, 'She is found by those who seek her.' and 'Whoever watches for her at dawn shall not be disappointed.'"

Little did he know, prayer would be just the ticket to deepen rather than clarify the burgeoning mystery.

Murderer in the Cathedral

Although it has largely fallen out of favor in the United States, a Catholic ritual called Exposition and Benediction was very popular in the 1940s. It involves a display of and procession with the Eucharist, unleavened bread that Catholics believe is miraculously transformed into the Body of Christ at Mass. A priest, garbed in especially ornate vestments, accompanied by at least two altar boys, carries the Eucharist in a gilded vessel called a monstrance. He then invites attendees to join him in prayers and songs of veneration. The rite was conducted entirely in Latin with a great deal of incense.

Medieval hits like "Tantum Ergo" and "O, Salutaris" were sung by all the kneeled participants. Benediction could be held almost anytime but was most often done on the first Friday of every month. Fridays were also marked by abstaining from meat, fasting, and a detailed recollection of Christ's suffering called The Stations of the Cross. Pre-Vatican II Catholics tended to focus much more heavily on the day of Christ's crucifixion than on his resurrection.

When Dorothy could find the time, she went to confession and benediction. Tamar often accompanied her. Although they usually worshiped in their neighborhood parish, when they had outings in midtown, they went to Saint Patrick's Cathedral. The Neo-Gothic church, dedicated in 1879 and located on Fifth Avenue directly across from Rockefeller Center, is the seat of the archbishop of the Roman Catholic Archdiocese of New York who is also the vicar for all American Catholics in the military. In 1941, that seat was occupied by Archbishop Francis Spellman, a man who believed war was a patriotic duty and Communists were the Church's mortal enemies.

Spellman did not have much use for union agitators or antiwar Catholics, and he had even less for conscientious objectors. He would later be known as one of the most outspoken supporters of the Vietnam War, calling it a "war for civilization" and "Christ's war." On one of several visits to Southeast Asia, Spellman cited Stephen Decatur: "My country, may it always be right, but right or wrong, my country." Dorothy and Spellman were bound by faith but miles apart in politics. On one occasion he suggested that she drop the word Catholic from the newspaper's masthead. When she did not do so, he dropped the matter. Not long after World War II, she criticized the by-then cardinal for bringing in seminarians as "scabs" to take the place of striking diocesan grave diggers. Despite their differences, Dorothy showed him respect and once proclaimed that, if the cardinal ordered her to close the Catholic Worker, she would obey him. Late in life, when asked why he didn't close the pacifist community, Spellman quipped, "Do you think I want to go down in history as the one who suppressed a saint?"

It irritated Dorothy when others summed her up in such lofty terms she always tried to dispel. She famously chided those who called her a saint, "Don't let yourself off so lightly." The saints were enormously important to her as very human examples of how to carry out God's will on earth. To many Catholics, however, saints loomed as plaster, god-like figures existing in ether way above us all.

"Is it true you have ecstasies and visions?" someone asked Dorothy.

"Yes," she answered. "Visions of unpaid bills." In the same vein, when volunteers came and wanted simply to talk about how much they admired the Catholic Worker, Dorothy often thrust a broom or paint brush into their hands and counseled them to work while they talked.

The Dorothy-is-a-saint notion was also hard on Tamar, who was often bombarded with questions about whether she was going to follow in her mother's footsteps. The almost unbearable pressure blotted out any chance that Tamar would be noticed in an individual way. It's small wonder that children of icons like Mahatma Gandhi had to struggle with their identity. Some were so bitter about growing up in a parent's shadow that they rebelled in shocking ways. When she thought about it, Tamar was grateful that Jesus had no children. As difficult as it was being in Dorothy's shadow, Tamar imagined it would be infinitely worse to be in Jesus' much longer shadow.

Smoldering resentment at the spillover from Dorothy's fame may have contributed to Tamar's less-than-enthusiastic embrace of religion. She went to Catholic schools, learned the prayers, and attended the ceremonies but never really took the faith to heart. To Dorothy's great regret, Tamar was destined to become a lapsed Catholic.

And so, while her mother knelt with her eyes closed in prayer, Tamar's gaze wandered the glorious church. Vast, filled with sculpture, stained glass, and people from every walk of life, Saint Patrick's Cathedral could just as easily distract a person from prayer as draw someone to it. Flexing her intertwined fingers absently like the wings of bird, Tamar scanned the vaulted ceiling. She then began to pick out individuals in the pews and tried to guess their occupations. A woman in pearls and a coat with a fur collar looked like a socialite. A gentleman in a three-piece suit, a banker. A woman all in black, an old maid or widow, perhaps a librarian. A boy in an uncomfortable-looking tweed jacket, a newsie dragged to church by his mother. A man nodding off to sleep in second-hand clothes, one of the thousands with bread and soup in his belly from someplace like—if not actually —the Catholic Worker.

Just as Tamar began really to enjoy her attempt to employ Sherlock Holmes's elementary method of deduction, she gasped to see Mr. New Shoes walk right by her pew, genuflect, and kneel two rows closer to the altar. Thanking God that the Catholic Church at that time insisted that women cover their heads in church, Tamar obscured her face by lowering her hat and raising her hands as if in prayer. Sneaking a peek through open fingers, Tamar spied on the possible murderer who, from all outward appearances, seemed to be really praying, a task that Tamar knew from personal experience could be faked.

"What is he doing here?" she wondered. "Was it a coincidence or had they been followed? Was her mother a potential target because of her support for unions? Was Tamar in his cross hairs for scrutinizing him at Saint Joe's?"

Before she could begin to answer those questions, he muddied the water even more by crossing himself, getting up slowly, genuflecting again, and heading toward one of the confessional boxes along the cathedral's exterior wall. He opened the door and stepped inside without looking back in Tamar's direction.

"Hobo, labor agitator, dock worker, and now penitent Catholic," Tamar marveled. "This guy's a regular Lon Chaney."

As the congregation began to sing, Tamar joined in while keeping half an eye on the confessional.

"Just what is this brute's game?" she asked herself.

Adding a deeper layer to the mystery, she saw him slip out, return to his pew, and bury his head in his hands. It wasn't hard to see that he was agitated, maybe even sobbing. If he was acting, he was pretty darned good at it.

Lifeboat Ethics

Hours later, after treating Tamar to hamburgers, fries, and ice cream in the shiny confines of the Empire Diner on Tenth Avenue, Dorothy insisted that Tamar attend the Catholic Worker's Friday night meeting. The gatherings responded to Peter's call for round-table discussions bringing workers and scholars together for "clarification of thought." Although Peter would have conducted them every night, the presentations came to be scheduled only once a week on Fridays. They featured little-known figures, activists, academics, and theologians as well as prominent speakers. As Dorothy and the Worker gained notoriety, it became almost a badge of honor to have led a discussion among the motley assortment of rascals who attended on Mott Street. More than once, someone robbed a speaker on the way to or from the engagement. Anyone who spent the night had to put up with bedbugs. Such trials only added to the allure for those who believed that the Catholic Worker was on the cutting edge of Catholic social action and spirituality. A lot of sins could be expunged by time at Saint Joseph's, especially in an age when Catholics routinely saw unmerited suffering as a ticket to redemption.

The French philosopher Jacques Maritain gave the talk Tamar previously attended. Maritain, a favorite of Dorothy's, spoke extremely poor English, and few of the attendees, save Peter, could understand what he said. Tonight featured A. J. Muste, a Protestant minister who had recently published the book *War Is the Enemy*. Hosting a minister was remarkable, considering that, in those days, Catholics would never sing Protestant songs nor even cross the threshold of a YMCA lest they risk being brainwashed into abandoning "the one true faith."

But the Catholic Worker wasn't a typical Catholic institution. In fact, Dorothy and Peter liked to call it an organism rather than an organization. Catholic Workers rubbed shoulders with blacks, Asians, Jews, Protestants, Communists, and all manner of people. The Worker welcomed Muste because he figured as a leading member of the Social Gospel movement. Soon after its founding, he joined the ecumenical Fellowship of Reconciliation, a group that proclaimed, "There is no way to peace. Peace is the way." A fellow who looked for all the world like an undertaker, Muste would go on to gain recognition as one of the most prominent American peace activists of the 1950s and 1960s.

Dorothy had high expectations for Muste's talk. He did not disappoint when he opened with the provocation, "If you cannot love Adolf Hitler, you cannot love."

The crowd, including a few American Jews and several refugees from Nazi Germany, took immediate offense. Only when Dorothy insisted on quiet could Muste continue. After first defining God's love as unfailing despite our unworthiness, he reminded the audience of Jesus's teaching, personal example, and final command: "Love one another as I have loved you."

"Unlike secular love," Muste said, "Christian love must be unselfish and unconditional, no matter how despicable an opponent might be." With all of Europe save Britain under the boot of the Third Reich, Muste proposed a very tough love to imagine, much less practice. It implied that Christians had to be willing to die rather than kill. Such talk had the capacity to sober an audience, to say the least.

Tamar resisted Muste's message. While she didn't expect to run into Mr. Hitler, she had plenty of experience with unlovable people. Over the years, she had amassed a few belongings of importance to her: a collection of seashells, some books, a couple of dolls, a doll house, a chemistry set, and a microscope. Some she had found, and Dorothy, Forster, or others gave her the rest. All of her treasures had been stolen no matter where she hid them in her fourth-floor bedroom at Saint Joseph's. The thieves may not have qualified as Nazis, but anyone who would steal from a little girl came mighty close to one in Tamar's book.

Dorothy provided a good example of detachment from personal possessions as well as dramatic forgiveness for reprehensible behavior of guests and volunteers. She inspired others to hold back their temper. Tamar remembered how decent Ade had been after an idiot from Fordham University had gone on a cleaning spree and scrubbed one of her murals off the wall. In contrast to Ade,

Tamar wanted to smack that guy on the side of his head and demand, "*What* in the world were you thinking?"—an ironic response, given Tamar's own inclination toward forgiveness when a disturbed and jealous guest stole her clothing and destroyed her collection of natural specimens. But then again, we always find it easier to forgive transgressions aimed at us rather than at our loved ones.

Indeed, when people you are trying to help steal personal possessions—items of no value to anyone but you—it's hard not to think of them as fiends. When they steal resources and tools and you need to serve them nevertheless, it's even harder not to see them as pains in the ass. Loving a distant enemy like Hitler poses a conceptually arduous problem. Loving a hurtful person who lives with you challenges even more. In the face of especially difficult guests, some Catholic Workers just snap. After a few years on Mott Street, John Cort concluded, "Trying to change some people by personal example is like throwing peanuts at a Sherman tank."

In the 1970s at the Catholic Worker farm in Hubbardston, Massachusetts, Jeanette Noel processed fruit she planted to make strawberry jam for Christmas presents to supporters. Upon returning from a short errand, she discovered that a guest had traded the two dozen Mason jars for a couple of quarts of Black Label beer. As Kurt Vonnegut says in *Slaughterhouse Five*, "Birdsong rings out alone in the silence after a massacre, 'Poo-tee-weet.'"

While Tamar grappled with Muste's message, Peter paid no attention to it at all. Pacifism wasn't part of his program, although he wasn't against it either. Keeping on guard for an opening to make a point, Peter discreetly surveyed the crowd for newcomers he might accost.

One of those newbies, a middle-aged woman, perhaps a housewife, interrupted Muste, "I can understand the morality of not killing to defend myself, but what about my children? Isn't it justifiable to kill to defend them?"

Before Muste could reply, a zealous Catholic Worker volunteer cited Luke 14:16: "If anyone comes to me and does not hate his father and mother, his wife and children, his brothers and sisters—yes, even his own life—he cannot be my disciple."

The bitterly familiar text hit Tamar hard. She had heard it ad nauseam from Father John Hugo during and after his excruciating retreats each summer at the Easton farm. Dorothy and a few others had embraced his message of total self-denial, though everyone did not. Stanley, keenly aware of how hard the lives of the poor and Catholic Worker volunteers already were, accused Father Hugo of "afflicting the afflicted."

Father Joseph Woods, a young Benedictine priest who stayed at Bowery flophouses when visiting the Worker, thought Father Hugo's retreat was only proper during Lent.

Tamar called it cruel and said, "The only good thing that came of it was that Dorothy quit smoking."

As a person who shared her father's wonder for the natural world and a child who had already been deprived of so much parental attention, Tamar could hardly be expected to embrace Hugo's view that "the best thing to do with the best things in life is to give them up." Telling her mother, who already spent most of her time away from her only child, that

God wanted her to be an even less attentive parent seemed monstrously callous.

And so, Tamar was understandably filled with trepidation when Dorothy rose to offer her view of the text.

Turning to the housewife, Dorothy said, "I am often asked, 'What would you do, if an armed maniac were to attack you, your child, or your mother?'"

After allowing the seriousness of the question to sink in, she continued, "Restrain him, of course, but not kill him. Confine him if necessary. But perfect love casts out fear, and love overcomes hatred." And then she added, "All this sounds trite, but experience is not trite."

Like a condemned man who gets a reprieve, Tamar was relieved to hear that her mother would not stand idly by as if watching her daughter being murdered were just another sacrifice to be embraced.

After nodding in agreement with Dorothy, Muste said, "We mustn't be fooled by hypothetical situations that violence is the only alternative to disaster. Reality is never that limited. Along with the Communists, Catholic Workers protested in 1935 against the creation of the first Nazi concentration camps. Hitler could have been stopped then by diplomatic means. Even now, we must not despair of finding a way to be at once apostles of peace *and* defenders of justice."

But then, who should stand up but Mr. New Shoes? No one knew he had attended the talk. No one saw him in the room till he got up to ask, "But wouldn't lives be saved by killing Hitler?"

"It certainly didn't work that way after Brutus assassinated Caesar," Dorothy answered.

Still standing, New Shoes said absently, "Unintended consequences."

"Indeed," Muste agreed, "There is so much we don't know. For example, how do we know when we kill a murderer that he was not destined to become another Saint Paul? After all, even that great evangelist could only see through a glass darkly."

At this, Muste pointed to a Columbia University grad student who had raised his hand, but before he could speak, New Shoes continued, "But aren't we justified to kill when the evidence is incontrovertible that our actions will prevent catastrophe? After all, the sailor in charge of a lifeboat full to capacity has no choice but to leave men, women, and even children in the water to drown."

After the grad student waved his hand in assent and retook his seat, Muste proffered, "When a string of tethered mountaineers dangles from a precipice and their combined weight is too great to pull themselves to safety, standard logic demands that at least one individual must be sacrificed to prevent the demise of the entire group."

New Shoes nodded, and Muste went on, "In such dire circumstance, the urgency to cut the rope is enormous, over-powering even. To do otherwise would be foolhardy, irresponsible, something we cannot imagine God would demand of us. And yet, the absurd poetry of the Gospel whispers, 'Be not afraid,' encouraging us to sheath our knives."

Dissatisfied, New Shoes fell back into his seat.

Astonished at the exchange, Peter scratched his chin while Tamar shrugged her shoulders.

Before either one could approach the other, though, Mr. Finlay, a frequenter of Friday night programs, sprang up shouting, "You'll never get me to love the Brits! I know damn well where I'd plant my knife. Killing is none too good for them, if you ask me!"

An Irishman, who played a minor role in the 1917 Easter Rebellion, Finlay was a seething mass of bitterness not unlike the hot-tempered racist and anti-Semite, Edward Breen, whose last words to Dorothy were "After I'm dead, I want you to take my cane and wrap it around the necks of all the bastards around here."

Dorothy moved to soothe Finlay, but before she could, another guest rose to denounce the "Eye-talians" and a general commotion ensued. By the time Finlay finally sat down with his arms fiercely folded and a semblance of order restored, the curious Mr. New Shoes had disappeared.

Patience and Fortitude

Tamar rose early on Saturday, entered the sparsely-occupied dining room, filled a bowl with oatmeal from an enormous pot, and sat down. Newcomers to the Catholic Worker often found it difficult to eat, considering the pervasive smell that no amount of bleach could eradicate. It was an aroma peculiar to those who seldom changed their clothes or bathed. You smelled it in tenements where mold, mildew, and the odor of cheap alcohol and cabbage prevailed. Cockroaches skittered not only across the floors and walls, but also on the tables and even plates of diners. Bedbugs assured that sleep would be intermittent. So tormented had a teenaged neighbor been by the pests that he doused his bed with alcohol and set it afire to kill them, only to burn half his building down. Lice were another cross to bear. Rats roamed without fear. Holes in the walls, filled with plaster mixed with broken glass and nails, were small impediments. Tamar remembered one Evening Prayer when a huge rodent stood on his hind legs between her and Dorothy as if he were curious what they were about.

And yet, for the most part, Tamar had fond memories of the Catholic Worker's early years. The idealism of the volunteers and supporters was infectious. She marveled to see Catholic Workers taking on more and more even as their funds became scarcer and scarcer. When bill collectors could not be put off another minute, Tamar remembered going to the Church of the Most Precious Blood to picket before the statue of Saint Joseph for funds. It was a day-to-day miracle that so many people got fed and so many newspapers got printed and distributed on nothing more substantial than faith.

But the Catholic Worker farm in Easton was her greatest joy. Although Peter was disappointed that his ideal of work mixed with Mass, lectures, and lessons never really took off, he too was part of Tamar's joy at the farm. She remembered fondly how Peter responded to a fist fight between an ex-cop and the cook over an egg by pledging to give up eggs and milk for the remainder of the summer so more could be available for others. Tamar was also thrilled by the fresh air, fruit, vegetables, and, especially, the presence of cats, dogs, chickens, geese, sheep, goats, rabbits, cows, horses, and pigs. So enamored did Tamar become of animals that she took in strays and often asked not only for traditional pets like kittens or mice, but also exotic ones like a hedgehog. To celebrate her graduation from Saint Dorothy's Academy, her mother gave Tamar a goat sadly destined to be killed three years later, in an ironic twist, by what Dorothy called a pack of homeless dogs.

At Easton, the cantankerous Mr. O'Connell, who was also a skilled carpenter, built a snug cabin with fifty-eight dollars Tamar had saved from Christmas and birthday gifts from her father. O'Connell located the cabin near a raspberry patch and orchard and deliberately made it scarcely large enough for a bunk bed, table, and chair so that only Dorothy and Tamar could stay there. Another volunteer, John Filigar, taught Tamar all he knew about farming. At Easton, Tamar came the closest to God. Her first confession was heard in 1938 by Father Woods, a priest with a glass eye, while she sat on a rock at the top of a hill overlooking the Delaware Water Gap and the Poconos. To Tamar, Maryfarm was a cathedral every bit as worthy as Saint Patrick's. When she wasn't in school, she would slip away to Easton any time she could.

Even in winter, during the few days before she had to return to boarding school, she would normally visit Easton. But the mystery held her back. She couldn't let it go. Who was this complicated man she called Mr. New Shoes? Could an earnest Christian be a cold-blooded murderer? Plenty of decent people, even some Catholic Workers, had enlisted in the military since the Japanese sneak attack in Hawaii. Peter Maurin himself had been in the French military, although not in combat. It was apparent that many human beings, police officers for example, could kill people in the line of duty without sacrificing their general decency. Maybe they kept the lethal part of their lives in a strongbox, securely separated from the rest of their daily lives.

It all seemed to Tamar at once probable and wacky, like the one-time guest at Saint Joe's who routinely stole items and promptly forgot where she had stowed them away. After that kleptomaniac volunteered to help find the culprit, it became obvious that she had no conscious awareness that the thief was herself. Or maybe Mr. New Shoes self-identified as some kind of crusader killing for a noble cause. A cop who puts a bullet in a gangster during a shoot-out wears that killing as a badge of honor. Most people would call him a hero, as they call most soldiers. The more Tamar thought, the more possibilities arose. The puzzle had a paucity of pieces. Perhaps, the expedition she planned would fill in some of the gaps.

Tied down as she was after her long speaking tour, Dorothy assented to Tamar's request to spend the morning by herself at the public library. Located at Fifth Avenue and Forty-Second Street adjacent to Bryant Park, New York City's main branch was not only a gorgeous Beaux-Arts masterpiece in marble but also the fourth largest library in the world. Dorothy had taken Tamar there at first to get books to read aloud and then, as Tamar grew older, to read on her own. Like all parents, Dorothy wanted her daughter to aim high with the classics while Tamar preferred Jane Austen's romance, Mark Twain's humor, and HG Wells's imagination to Dostoevsky's and Tolstoy's grim moralizing. Truth be told, her favorites were the Ruth Fielding novels about a strong-willed British orphan who overcomes every obstacle in her unconventional desire to pursue a career. Like the Nancy Drew books to follow them, the Fielding novels were formula books written by various authors under pseudonyms. They were a relief for Tamar from the suffocating options presented to her by society. Like her mother, Tamar did not want to be told what she could and could not do. Unfortunately, Dorothy considered the popular series trash, thus forcing Tamar to read them surreptitiously.

After bundling up for the cold and making sure she had two buffalo nickels for subway tokens, Tamar turned right outside Saint Joseph's and walked past the ten-foot-high walls of the Old Saint Patrick's Cathedral cemetery to catch an uptown train on Canal Street to Grand Central Station. Unlike the so-called new Saint Patrick's Cathedral in Midtown, Old Saint Patrick's opened in 1815 on Mulberry Street in the Lower East Side. It served at the Archbishop's seat until the larger cathedral opened in 1879.

While bumping along underground, she mused on the concept of vocation. Her mother clearly had found hers and was anxious that Tamar do so as well. In her Newport studio, Ade told Tamar that, before she could choose a vocation, she had to discover her own identity. Father Pacifique Roy, a Canadian priest who organized interracial basketball games in Montreal, told Tamar, "The only thing necessary is love."

The nuns at Saint Dorothy's, a school filled with the children of widows, widowers, and single working parents, had counseled Tamar to take up something that made her happy.

The contrary Father Hugo considered making oneself happy self-indulgent and told retreatants that instead they should take up something they did not want to do. Thankfully, for her peace of mind, Tamar had already set his approach aside. During her short stint as a scholarship student at Oak Hill, a school favored by the daughters of Hollywood moguls, Tamar witnessed how miserable a person could be if forced to live against her nature.

All parents, rich and poor, want to shield their offspring from grief and hop skip them without delay to what they believe to be the best life for them to lead. By the time parents realize that the approach is more likely to alienate teenagers than make them grateful, it's often too late to make amends. Perhaps the best definition of adulthood is the time when we can at last forgive our parents.

Such thoughts drew Tamar's attention to one wonderfully bad idea of Dorothy's. In hope of spending more time with Tamar to whom she really was devoted, Dorothy enrolled her in Transfiguration High School on Mott Street, only a few blocks from St. Joe's. Instead of boarding Monday through Friday at Saint Dorothy's on Staten Island and restricting their time together to the weekends, the new school allowed Tamar to room with Dorothy at the Catholic Worker, attend early Mass with her each day, and work on homework together at the library. They even found time to walk along the East River or down to Battery Park and look across the harbor at the Statue of Liberty. In time though, the chronic poverty of the Catholic Worker compelled Dorothy to travel again and again.

Nonetheless, the Mott Street school continued to seem like a good choice, that is until Tamar was courted by a young man named Dwight Larrowe. So enamored was the boy that he asked fifteen-year-old Tamar to marry him, prompting Dorothy to transfer Tamar after only one week's training in French to a distant school in Montreal. Not to be thwarted, Dwight wrote to Tamar in Canada and sent her books that Dorothy would probably never buy. The romance was not destined to endure, but the resentment at being yanked out of yet another school by a controlling, even if well-meaning, parent was hard to forgive.

Before she could stew about her adolescent chafing at being told what to do at the advanced age of fifteen, the conductor called out her stop. Tamar gathered her bag and trundled her way up to New York's iconic Grand Central train station. Out she rushed onto the street and then two blocks west to Fifth Avenue where the New York Public Library rises like a Roman or Greek temple. Were it not for pushcarts loaded with steaming chestnuts and pretzels for sale, she might have longed to don suitable ancient attire.

After nodding to the marble lion named Patience reclining at the south end edge of the staircase, Tamar stroked the paw of its sibling, Fortitude. Encouraged by the way the beast's head turned ever so slightly in her direction, Tamar could believe she had his protection. Wasting no time, she hustled up the stairs and into the Rose Reading Room whose large curved windows, massive chandeliers, high ceiling with elaborate wood carving encircling a painting of swirling clouds, and rows of sturdy and ornate tables each with its own table lamps gave Tamar the feeling that she was in a royal library. It was so beautiful that she always liked to claim a spot there even before she found a book to read.

After securing a seat with her canvas bag, Tamar hastened to the periodical room only to learn that the library's policies wouldn't allow her to bring newspapers to the reading room from that less-impressive space. Impatient to get to work and not at all concerned for her bag, Tamar began scanning papers for more news about Fitzpatrick and Veronica's murders. In no time at all, she amassed a pile of no fewer than twelve daily papers and six weeklies. Ranging in price from two cents for *The Daily Mirror* and *Daily News* to seven cents for the

Wall Street Journal, none sold for as little as a penny a copy
as *The Catholic Worker* did. All of them were densely packed
with news, sometimes six columns across on each page with
few photographs or illustrations. Some, like *The New York Post*
and *The New York Star*, featured glaring headlines, but most
undersold their stories. Many, like the leading Negro weekly,
The New York Age, catered to particular communities. Tamar
wondered, "How in the world do New Yorkers sustain so
many papers?" And more importantly, "How will I ever find
anything in this mountain of news?"

Over the next hour, Tamar found many things. Unfortunately, none of them related to the murders. She encoun-
tered loads of contradictory news from the Pacific where the
United States was either on its heels against the Japanese
or driving them back with ease. Franklin Roosevelt pressed
for more troops, more ships, more tanks, and less delay.
The British prime minister, Winston Churchill met the US
president at the Arcadia Conference in Washington, DC, and
urged no quarter for the Nazis and the Japanese.

In Albany, Governor Lehman, a Democrat, Reform Jew,
and big fan of Roosevelt's New Deal, announced that both of
his sons, Peter and John, had enlisted in the military. Mayor
La Guardia, an Italian-American Republican with a Jewish
mother and lapsed Catholic father, continued to urge rescue
of Jewish refugees and swift action against Hitler, whom he
called a "brown-shirted fanatic."

Joe DiMaggio, who hit in 56 consecutive games, batted
.357 for the season, and led the Yankees over the Dodgers
in the 1941 World Series, announced he was going to enlist
as had a number of sports and movie stars. Some questioned

whether baseball should continue at all during the war. All very interesting, but none of it relevant to the mystery.

Tamar's neck began to ache and her eyes burn by the time she read in an Irish independence weekly, *The Gaelic American*:

> Thomas Fitzpatrick, the son of the former chief of staff of the Irish Republican Army and Clann na Poblachta politician Mick Fitzpatrick, was murdered on December 29 in New York City's Gramercy Park. The young Fitzpatrick had been an organizer for the IWW.

"There it is!" Tamar said aloud before being shushed by a disapproving librarian.

Not long after, she learned that the body of another man with a slashed throat had been discovered on New Year's Eve in an alley only three blocks south of St. Joseph's. He was identified as James Hartley, a professor of ancient philosophy at Fordham University. According to the medical examiner, Hartley's murder had most likely occurred three days earlier.

Realizing that Hartley could have been killed on the twenty-eighth before or after New Shoes's appearance at the Catholic Worker, Tamar wondered, "Why in the world would anyone murder a philosophy teacher?" Then she remembered that, in the Christian calendar, the twenty-eighth of December recalls the day King Herod sent troops to kill all the newborn children in Bethlehem. It is the Feast of the Slaughter of the Holy Innocents.

Time to Confer

Eager to share her discoveries with Peter, Tamar grabbed her bag and took the subway down to Union Square where, sure enough, he was in full swing. Despite her impatience, Tamar sat at a nearby bench and watched as the short man spoke with obvious passion. His face, lined with wrinkles, conveyed a nobility that a passerby might miss. Wearing his only suit of clothing, having slept the previous night-as every night prior to it-in whatever available nook that didn't displace another person, Peter was easy to underestimate.

Tamar knew that when a professor invited Peter to his home for dinner, the professor's wife mistook him for the gas meter reader and ushered him into the cellar where he remained without complaint until the professor arrived. When Peter chaired a four-day conference in Chicago, he slept on a bench at the Greyhound station the first three nights and, at the organizer's insistence, spent the final night in a guest room reserved for the bishop at Saint Ignatius Rectory. Tamar recognized Peter as authentic. Every idea he promulgated he himself first and foremost put into practice. The warm glow in Peter's eyes and his animated gestures so moved Tamar that she listened contentedly rather than interrupt him.

"I am not afraid of the word Communism," he said to the small crowd, "At the same time, I am not opposed to private property with responsibility. But those who own private property should never forget it is a trust."

He went on to say that we needed to "shift civilization from contracts to contacts," an idea that very much appealed to his audience and to Tamar.

In response to a listener's suggestion that, in a democratic society such as the United States, citizens have a patriotic duty to defend the country and its system, Peter replied, "To stand up for one's country when one's country is wrong does not make the country right. To stand up for the right, even when the world is wrong, is the only way I know of to make everything right."

Because Dorothy was destined to live until 1980 whereas Peter's health would gradually decline until his death in 1949, most living members of the Catholic Worker movement have no memory of him. Their entire impression of Peter often derives exclusively from his easy essays, but those, while an excellent introduction to his thinking, only scratch the surface of his remarkable perspective and life story. For example, Peter so eagerly wanted to confront racial discrimination that in 1942 he and a friend started a house of hospitality in Harlem. Years earlier, Peter had knocked on a stranger's door to ask for a drink of water. Neighbors mistook him for a burglar, and Peter spent a week in jail. He knew that, if he had been black, police may have shot him or the neighbors may have lynched him.

As the only white residents in their Harlem neighborhood, Peter and his friend endured quite a bit of rejection and drew very few people to their meetings for clarification of thought, but Peter was undeterred. He knew that the Depression hit blacks especially hard and that Catholics had done little to address their plight. He went so far as to appear at Harlem's storied Apollo Theater to try and get his message out. Unfortunately, the playbill listed him as a comedian and, not long after he started talking, the crowd booed so loudly he was given the hook. Yet, when a black soldier was shot by a white policeman and Harlem erupted in riots, rioters smashed the windows of most storefronts but not those of the Harlem Catholic Worker. Respected members of the neighborhood told the mob that Peter and his friend "were good people."

As impressed as she was with Peter, Tamar began to get pretty cold.

Maurin, on the other hand, had just warmed up, as he railed about how the mortgage industry had "become an octopus strangling the life of our people" and how "we need gentle personalists and not rugged individualists."

Tamar caught his eye, clapped her arms around her body, stamped her feet, and made an exaggerated display of shivering. A smile crossed Peter's face. He had gotten her message.

With a sincere promise to return and generous distribution of books he had stuffed in his coat pockets, Peter made a graceful, if somewhat abrupt, exit.

"Bonjour, Tamar," he said with a broad smile.

"Bonjour, to you, too, Peter," Tamar replied, "but I think it would be an even better day if we could get out of the cold to talk."

"But of course," he agreed as they both hustled out of the square and toward a tea shop about half way to Saint Joe's.

Since they had only fifteen cents between them, they could afford just two cups of tea. Considering the frigid temperature, hot drinks provided all they needed. Once comfortably situated in a cozy chair opposite Peter with her still gloved hands embracing a steaming cup of tea, Tamar summarized what she had learned at the library.

Peter listened intently, gave his head a characteristic tilt, and asked, "So, if we assume these three unfortunates were killed by the same person, we must ask ourselves, 'What do they have in common?'"

After a pause, he continued, "Only the professor may have been carrying more than one or two dollars, so it's safe to say that theft can be ruled out. "

Taking up from there, Tamar said, "The Wobbly could easily have had enemies but not foes who target unpublished poets or teachers of Plato and Socrates."

"Précisément," Peter concurred. "And yet, while it is not obvious to us, the killer sees a link among his victims. If Monsieur Nouvelles Chaussures is the killer, I am convinced he does it with one purpose in mind."

"I agree," said Tamar. "His appearances in the soup line as a vagrant and in Union Square as a Russian laborer don't seem random, but turning up at Saint Patrick's as a penitent and the Friday night meeting as someone struggling with the morality of violence suggest he is conflicted."

Peter nodded, sipped some tea, and said, "Conflicted? Perhaps." Peter sipped some more and added darkly, "Deterred? I do not think so."

As often occurred with much of his visionary thinking, events would vindicate Peter's observations.

Murder Most Urgent

Time was running out. Thirteen knew it. Unless he acted in the next thirty-six hours, all he had done would be for naught. Until now, he had only been nibbling at the edges of his mission. Each death increased the probability of ultimate success but none as significantly as the demise of the victim he had saved for last. Without her, the calamity he had been sent to prevent would still occur. She represented the keystone supporting the entire edifice that had to be demolished.

Since Thirteen understood the scenario as obvious, why didn't he act without delay? Part of the reason concerned the fact that his target seemed virtually never to be alone. Yet, he acknowledged the idea as a lame excuse. Not even the most social figures, from Christ to Gandhi, lived without times in solitude. Truth be told, he needed reassurance. A. J. Muste's and Dorothy Day's naïve words nevertheless touched a nerve. He wished he could have asked many more questions. Maybe their answers or lack thereof would have given him peace of mind.

"Probably not," he said aloud. "How could they begin to understand what is at stake?"

No, there were no alternatives. He had to kill Dorothy Day—and very soon. And the road to accomplish the murder led straight to her daughter.

Thirteen Strikes

Once back at Mott Street, Tamar parted company with Peter, said hello to Dorothy, and went up to their room on the fourth floor. No one else was there, providing Tamar an opportunity to mull over the available clues and devise a plan to gain more of them. Like Agatha Christie's master detective, Hercule Poirot, she planned to sit down and exercise her "little grey cells." Before she could construct such a mind castle, a loud crash startled her. Fearing the worst, she spun around only to see the kitten her mother had given her for Christmas running away from an overturned table by the back window. Relieved and embarrassed, Tamar walked over and bent down to set things right. As she straightened up, though, with her hair brushing up against the window glass, she looked with horror straight into the face of Mr. New Shoes. Aghast, she pulled back, only to realize he was moving to open the window, a task he could accomplish only because she stood too far away to lock it.

Knowing from past experience in their raucous home and neighborhood that a scream would arouse little notice, she rushed to the downstairs door which, unlike the offending window, stuck and refused to open. Just as the door began to budge, the villain thrust one arm firmly to hold the wooden door and the other around Tamar's neck. Scratching furiously at his nasty arm with both of her hands, she managed to wriggle free long enough to grab what she hoped was a claw hammer. It turned out to be a feather duster. What in the world was such a foolish thing like that doing in their room? she wondered even as she thrust it into New Shoes' open mouth. During his momentary confusion, she unsuccessfully sought another means of defense.

He tossed aside the duster and said, "I salute you, Miss Day, for your feisty nature." A lesser person would have fainted straightaway. His comment almost made her laugh since for many years during school at Saint Dorothy's, she had a habit of fainting for no apparent reason.

Instead, she said, "A lesser person would not have figured out what you are up to either."

Of all things he had imagined, her reply did not qualify as one of them. Dumbfounded for several seconds, he recovered with, "You're bluffing. You couldn't possibly have the slightest idea what my mission is."

"True enough," she thought, but said instead, "You're not as clever as you think you are." She added, "Your 'mission' is as good as over."

If she could buy some time, maybe her mother or Stanley would show up.

Instead of answering, he withdrew a bottle from his right-hand pocket and a cloth from his left.

"Yikes!" she realized. He meant to chloroform her just like in the movies.

Completely grabbing at straws, Tamar said with as much conviction as she could muster, "You believe you can make something good come out of something evil. I may be only fifteen, but even I know that's a fool's errand."

"Are you trying to provoke me into killing you?" he demanded.

"If you were going to kill me," she hazarded, "you'd already have done so."

Amazed at her cheek and perception, he tipped the contents of the bottle onto the cloth and moved to cover her mouth with it.

"There will be consequences," she warned.

"In this case," she heard as he forced her to breath the noxious chemical and she began to lose consciousness, "I certainly hope not."

Final Arguments

Tamar woke to find herself tied to a chair in a small warehouse. New Shoes was seated at a desk with his back to her. He was looking at something by the light of a gooseneck lamp.

"Only three and a half hours left," he muttered.

Just then, the side door burst open and Peter shouted, "Have no fear, Tamar! I am here."

New Shoes reacted quickly as he pinned Peter's arms behind his back after only a momentary struggle and then tied him securely to a chair adjacent, but not too close, to Tamar's.

"And who the heck are you?" Thirteen asked.

"Aristide Pierre Maurin," Peter replied with dignity, "I am Tamar's friend."

Apparently, the girl was not the only one on his trail.

"New York is becoming quite a nuisance," Thirteen thought.

Meanwhile, Tamar scanned the abandoned desk for any clues as to New Shoe's motive and plan. To her surprise, the only object she saw was a slender black wristband. A faint glow emitted from the side she could not see. The first thing that came to Tamar's mind was, "It's a Dick Tracy two-way radio watch," even though she knew such things were pure fiction. Whatever it was, when New Shoes caught her staring at it, he swept the device into the desk drawer. Then, without a word, he began packing a small bag.

Tamar addressed Peter, "Our host is an ends-justifies-the-means fellow."

"Really?" Peter answered, "I took him to be more sophisticated."

Thirteen stopped abruptly and said, "The good of the many outweighs the good of the few."

Not to be outdone, Tamar countered, "The road to hell is paved with good intentions."

With a one-two punch, Peter, a great admirer of Judaism, quoted the Talmud: "Whoever destroys a soul destroys the entire world. And whoever saves a life saves the entire world."

His anger rising, Thirteen said, "When God ordered Abraham to kill his son Isaac, the patriarch obeyed without question."

"But that was only a test," Tamar said, "God stopped Abraham from actually killing Isaac."

"But God did not stop his angel from slaughtering the Egyptian children at Passover," Thirteen answered.

"You, Monsieur, are not an angel," Peter reminded, "Neither you nor I have a perfect understanding of God's will. Religious fanatics proclaiming that God told them when the world would end are a dime a dozen."

"You have a point there," Thirteen considered, "Nearly a thousand Jews at Masada endured mass murder and suicide rather than captivity by the Romans. And Reverend Jim Jones convinced more than nine hundred people to commit suicide. Was that God's will? The devil's? Or just plain insanity? Was David following God when he slew Goliath? Was Samson following the devil when he brought the temple down on his own and everyone else's head? Was Judith insane when she beheaded Holofernes?

"I put it to you, Monsieur Maurin," Thirteen continued. "How can you know for certain that your ideals are from God? How do you know you are not delusional?"

Straining her neck to see beyond their captor, Tamar asserted, "You have to admit, Peter, those are pretty good questions."

"Thank you," Thirteen said, glancing over his shoulder.

"Don't mention it," she replied.

Peter had not yet finished, but hampered by his inability to gesticulate, he struggled to free his hands. As he did so, another mighty crash turned all eyes toward the door filled with the determined form of Joe Zarella.

Exasperated, Thirteen asked, "And just who the bloody hell are you?"

Joe replied with considerable aplomb, "I am legion. For we are many."

Unfortunately, Joe stretched the truth about as far as possible. No one actually accompanied Joe, and, in pitifully short order, he joined his friends in captivity.

For the next few minutes, no one spoke. Thirteen returned to packing. From her vantage point, Tamar caught a glimpse of the last item he placed in the valise—a wickedly sharp-looking bone-handled knife. She also saw him remove the wristband from the drawer and put it on. During the quick exchange, she saw that a set of numbers blinked on its face. Although they showed upside down from her angle, she could tell they counted down. Certain the countdown constituted the key to the mystery, she racked her brain to unlock its significance.

While she struggled mentally, Peter renewed the debate by asserting, "The answer is love."

Thirteen looked up and asked, "What did you say?"

"You are right that we can never fully know God's will," Peter said, "God's knowledge is infinite. Ours is not. Our minds have limitations of all things physical, but our hearts are metaphysical. Because God has loved us so much, we can defy reason and love even those who hate us."

Unsure of what was going on, Joe nonetheless chimed in, "Peter is right. My decision to refuse to fight in this war is about as irrational as you can get, but I feel, deep in my heart, that I am called to refuse to fight. In a way, I cannot even accept a role as conscientious objector, because that would exempt me and not challenge the state's right to send others to war. It would imply my support for the war."

"With all due respect, Sir, the world is a stage and we are just players upon it," Thirteen retorted with bitter resignation. "My part is already written in God's book. My duty is to carry it out without question."

"No one is God's marionette." Joe said sympathetically, "God gave us all free will."

"As it says in Leviticus," Peter jumped in, "'I have set before you life and death. Choose life, therefore, that you and your descendants might live.'"

"And so," Thirteen said, "we have gone full circle. In order for my descendants to live, I must in actual fact choose death. As abhorrent as this may sound to you, it is the plain truth."

"Do not give up on yourself," Peter counseled. "Unlike Pilate, you must ask sincerely, 'What is truth?'"

Thirteen shook his head slowly and said, "It's too late." Before turning to leave, he added, "I have made provisions that you will be set free in the morning."

Just then, like the buzzer on an alarm clock, Tamar exclaimed, "I know who you are!"

"Please," Thirteen said. "Stop trying to stall me."

"No," she answered, "I really do know."

He paused on the threshold.

With conviction, she proclaimed, "You are the time traveler."

He raised his eyebrows and tipped his hat before saying, "Bravo and adieu."

The door closed behind him and all was silent.

No Choice

As Thirteen walked to Saint Joseph's, he marveled, "Who would have thought it? That girl read HG Wells's book and has the imagination to believe it could be true."

He almost wished he could have told her the entire story, but he didn't have time. In less than two hours, he would be whisked back to the year 2030. God willing, his actions will have averted disaster. Yet, like a stubborn splinter that resists removal, doubts nagged at him. For one thing, the problem of unintended consequences exists in every scenario. The scientists assured him that these murders increased the probability of the desired outcome by ninety percent, but would he play Russian roulette with a one-live-shell-in-ten shooter?

If he had to be honest, he wouldn't put a gun to his head with only one live bullet out of a hundred. The odds did not guarantee that the outcome would be better. The butterfly effect, which holds that the death of a single of those frail insects could result in a catastrophe somewhere else in the world, is the very reason time travel was outlawed in 2029. Who could blame Aleksandr Solzhenitsyn and other inmates of Soviet gulags for wishing Vladimir Lenin had never been born? After all, Solzhenitsyn had no idea that the Communist regime would fall and, after a period under strongmen like Vladimir Putin, Russia would embrace liberal democracy. Who can say what would have happened if Czar Nicholas II had not been killed?

The math really bothered Thirteen. A ninety percent chance of success sounded pretty good until he considered cases like Truman over Dewey, the '69 Mets, the '04 Red Sox, the '16 Cubs, and Trump over Clinton. And of course, after Jesus was arrested, stripped, tortured, and crucified, no one would have given decent odds that He'd make a comeback. In his novel *Imagining Argentina*, Lawrence Thornton posits that a mental conception of a good outcome, even in a dire circumstance, dramatically increases the likelihood that it will come to pass. What if one had to account for such intangibles? If every outcome relied exclusively on mathematical probability, no sane person would ever buy a lottery ticket. Computations might look good on paper, but in real life, variables are innumerable and consequences unpredictable.

On top of such mysterious imponderables, Thirteen had growing theological queries. Would a good God saddle humanity with a crisis only resolvable by violating the sixth commandment? Even if the bulk of humankind had become so corrupt as to deserve annihilation, Genesis tells us that only a handful of righteous people in Sodom would have held back God's wrath. And Jewish mystics talk about the Lamed Vav Tzadikim, a single just man in every generation for whose sake God is merciful to the entire human race.

Thirteen wondered, "Would a loving God torture a decent person like Job simply to win a bet against the devil? Would a merciful God say to Saul, 'Now go attack the Amalekites and totally destroy all that belongs to them. Do not spare them; put to death men and women, children and infants, cattle and sheep, camels and donkeys'"?

All the thinking gave Thirteen had a splitting headache. "Before you know it," he said aloud, "I'll be asking if God can make an object so heavy that God cannot lift it. I might as well go down the rabbit hole with Alice."

Despite the turmoil swirling inside him, Thirteen came ever closer to Mott Street. As with scientists at Los Alamos who suspected that the Trinity nuclear test would ignite the atmosphere in an omnicidal firestorm, inertia swept him along. While he did not want to join company with Judas, Robert Oppenheimer, and countless others who bitterly regretted their actions in their aftermath, he felt powerless to turn around.

Reaching into his bag, he grasped the handle of the knife, slipped it back inside, and, to reassure himself, cited Martin Luther: "Here I stand, I can no other, so help me God."

In Pursuit

Back in Thirteen's warehouse, Joe broke the silence. "Mr. Smarty Pants may be able to tie a pretty tight knot, but he knows nothing about frisking a person."

After he wriggled a bit, a small pocket knife slid out of his sleeve. As it nearly landed on the floor, Joe caught it. Once he had a firm grip, he painstakingly opened it and positioned the blade over the rope binding his wrist. He carefully sawed back and forth for what seemed like an eternity before he freed his hands and began to release Tamar and Peter.

All of them felt urgency to get to Saint Joe's before their strange captor could kill anyone else, but Tamar wondered if it wouldn't be faster to find a telephone and call the police. Peter opposed the idea on principle. Joe reminded Tamar that, no matter how urgently she might beg for help, the police would not rush into Little Italy. Even if they did, they could just as easily injure or kill the wrong person as the right one.

"So, let's go," Tamar concluded.

"Wait a minute," Joe replied. "Your mother would never forgive us if we put you in harm's way. I'll go. I'm a fast runner and can beat him to Saint Joe's. Peter can escort you and keep you at a safe distance."

Before she could protest, Joe was out the door. Without indication of his intentions, Peter took Tamar's hand and led her outside as well, where they headed toward Mott Street at a trot.

To Joe's surprise when he arrived at the Catholic Worker, he found Dorothy herself facing off against danger, only her potential assailant was not the one he expected. When Joe burst into the soup kitchen, Stanley stopped him cold. The room was crowded but deathly quiet. An obviously very angry and very drunk sailor looked at a few of the men and shouted, "If you don't get out of here, I'll kill you!"

From Joe and Stanley's vantage point, it wasn't clear if the man was armed.

Dan Orr, a former policeman and truck driver who had lost everything in Depression-afflicted New York and arrived at the Worker wanting nothing more than to soak his tired feet, feared for Dorothy's life. He knew from experience how quickly a drunken rant could escalate.

Heedless of danger, Dorothy had left the food-serving line, approached the sailor, and said, "You are a great friend to us, and we are grateful, very grateful."

He looked at her with fierce blue eyes dancing. He dragged his right hand through his thick, curly hair, and then wiped it on his trousers as if he'd touched something dirty.

Seeing Dorothy follow his hand, he bellowed, "What the hell are you looking at?"

With incredible composure, she replied simply, "At you."

He shouted back, "Well, who are you?"

"I'm Dorothy Day," she replied. "And what is your name?"

"Fred," he replied.

Dorothy offered her hand to him.

He offered his, but before they could shake, he asked, "Aren't you worried that I'm dirty?"

"No," she answered. "I haven't washed my own hands. There's all kinds of crud on them from the kitchen. Can you excuse me?"

"Yes," he replied, and they shook.

Without losing the moment, Dorothy said, "Thank you. You have been a lifesaver," perhaps in gratitude for the respite he engendered from the crowd's typical din.

He gave her a strange look, then stared at the floor, and, without looking up at her, growled, "I don't want to be called a lifesaver."

The tension in the room grew almost unbearable. Fred's growling felt in many ways more frightening than his earlier rage. He seemed to be as tightly wound as a rattlesnake ready to strike at any second.

Incongruously, Dorothy asked, "May I give you some soup?"

"What's in it?" he demanded with suspicion.

"Lots of good vegetables," Dorothy answered with no more anxiety than if she had been a waitress answering one of her customers.

"Will you have some?" he asked.

"I sure will," Dorothy said. "I'm hungry."

After filling two bowls, she encouraged him to sit at an empty table across from her, but he seemed reluctant to start eating until she did, so she took a few tablespoons.

Somewhat mollified, he took a few tentative mouthfuls before asking, "Can I have your soup?"

"Sure," she agreed and switched the bowls, which encouraged him to eat with gusto for a bit until he abruptly stopped, stared into his bowl, and began growling once more.

Dorothy pressed on, "May I have your soup?"

"I want you to have it," he said.

Taking him at his word, she drew the bowl to her side of the table, lifted it, and ate all of it. When she put the bowl down, he stared at it. Dorothy broke the silence by asking, "Is there anything else you want?"

He didn't answer.

"I'm very happy to meet you, Fred," she said and then turned to another guest asking, "How are you doing?"

Before he could answer, the drunken man moved closer to Dorothy and barked like a dog. Everyone braced for violence. Again, Dorothy defied convention by looking towards Fred and smiling.

He did not smile back.

Undaunted, she picked up a piece of bread, broke it in half, took part of one half in her mouth, and offered the other half to him.

To everyone's relief, he took it and said, "Thank you."

Finally, as casually as she could manage, Dorothy said, "Oh, do come here, anytime. We'd love to have you as our guest. Now, please excuse me. I have to get some vegetables for tomorrow's soup."

Almost like magic, Fred returned to his seat, and, for that once, it was a great relief to hear the room gradually return to the familiar racket.

Joe was so relieved, he had completely forgotten about Thirteen, who was nowhere to be seen.

Peter, who arrived in time to see the drama, said to no one in particular, "That's what I call overcoming evil with good."

Face to Face

One thing about the Catholic Worker that helps its members deal with crises concerns the sheer volume of work and frequency of calamities. Day-to-day life is so full that little time remains to dwell on individual events. Like kids riding waves at the seashore, Workers learn to get up quickly lest the next wave catch them off guard. Dorothy had not simply put Fred off. She really did have to get carrots, potatoes, and onions for the next day's soup. During winter on the rare occasions of excess supplies, Workers often stowed them in boxes outside the back kitchen door. Unlike ubiquitous cardboard of the early twenty-first century, most things in the 1940s came in sturdy wooden crates that could withstand rats if not left unattended for long.

While Dorothy usually considered the din of many people eating and talking a cross to bear, on that night she found the resumption of noise heavenly. It spoke of normalcy. Fear had completely fled from her mind. All she could think of after the episode was collecting vegetables and then heading upstairs to spend some time with Tamar.

Threading her way around the cook, dishwasher, and assorted others ladling soup and handing out bread, Dorothy opened the door into the back alley. By then, it had grown pretty dark. As soon as she opened the door, a rush of cold air reminded her that winter had begun in earnest. With a small laugh, she said, "I sure have come a long way from California, Mexico, and Florida."

As the door swung closed behind her and she bent to inspect a crate, she was taken aback to hear a soft voice ask with emotion, "How could you do that?"

"Excuse me?" Dorothy asked before she saw the man who spoke to her. He wore a long coat and carried a valise.

"How could I do what?"

"I saw through the window how you responded to that drunk," he said. "He could have attacked you, even killed you, you know."

"But he didn't, did he?" she said.

"No," he agreed, "but that doesn't answer how you knew he wouldn't."

Matter-of-factly, she replied, "I didn't know. We never do."

"You have great faith," he marveled.

"I'm not so conceited as to think that highly of myself," she scoffed. "Each of us has a measure of faith God deals to us. All we can do is loathe evil and cling to the good."

When he didn't reply, she said, "I have to bring these crates inside. Can you please lend me a hand?"

"Certainly," he answered, setting his valise down to do so.

After they completed the task, Dorothy grasped both his hands in hers and invited him in to have soup and bread.

"Thank you," he said with feeling, "but I really must go."

"Well," she said. "Thank you for your help. And, please know that you too are always welcome here."

Five minutes later, after he had vanished down the alley, Dorothy noticed out the back-door window that he had left his valise behind.

Time Runs Out

His mind made up, Thirteen decided to spend his last minutes in 1941 sitting on the steps of Old Saint Patrick's Cathedral. The screaming match going on in his mind and conscience had ended. While he knew there could be no certainty, he no longer cared. So at ease had he become that he didn't hear Tamar approach.

Somehow, she intuited that he posed no danger and sat beside him.

As they sat in silence, it began to snow. Looking out at the slow-moving flakes illuminated by streetlights, she said, "It's beautiful."

"It certainly is," he agreed without stirring.

Five minutes passed before he said, "I suppose you'd like to know the full story."

"Only if you wish to share it," she answered.

"You deserve at least an outline," he said looking directly into her eyes. "You see, a few years hence, men will build terrifying nuclear weapons powerful enough to kill millions of people. As those weapons spread across the globe, they will threaten the very existence of life on the planet. There will be many near disasters. But people like your mother, the daughter of that poet, the son of that professor, and the granddaughter of that unionist as well as others in other cities will call for disarmament.

"For years, such peacemakers will manage to hold back but not reverse the threat of mass destruction. But in 2017, 122 nations will sign a treaty to abolish nuclear weapons. Led by a remarkable Catholic bishop from Detroit-a man deeply moved by your mother, by the way-peacemakers will press on until every nation ratifies the treaty and carries out its provisions. But, just as the world seems about to breathe a sigh of relief, a shadowy criminal organization will threaten to obliterate a different world capital each day until the organization can gain astronomical power and wealth. To emphasize the veracity of their threat, the villains will detonate a mega-bomb in the mid-Atlantic Ocean. Experts will locate their launch sites but realize that only another super-bomb could penetrate their defenses. Disarmament will have been so complete, no nation could reconstruct what they will consider necessary weapons in time. As the deadline looms for the first city's destruction, govern-ments will send thirteen men back in time to try and alter history in the way you now know I attempted. Despite the ease with which H. G. Wells's protagonist travels forward and backward through the ages, the process actually poses extreme difficulty and requires rare minerals and enormous energy. We thirteen constitute, most probably, the last human beings who will ever travel through time."

He paused and then concluded, "And with the choice that I have now made, we may also be among the last human beings on earth."

Tamar thought about his tale and offered, "You can't be sure of that."

"I know that now," he agreed.

"I may not have my mother's faith," Tamar said, "but I do have hope. Wasn't that the only thing left at the bottom of Pandora's box?"

"Yes, it was," he said with a smile.

Just then, the band on his wrist began to emit a beeping noise.

Thirteen, stood up and said, "I'm afraid it's time for me to go."

"May I ask you one last question?" she said.

"Certainly," he replied.

"What is your name?"

"John," he said and then offered his hand. "It was a singular pleasure to meet you, Tamar."

She shook and replied, "In a roundabout way, I'm glad I met you, too, John."

Almost immediately after she withdrew her hand, he vanished.

The Unexpected

The following day, Tamar slept in. When she finally went downstairs, the first people she met were Peter and Stanley. They were both almost ecstatic.

"And just what has happened to make you two so gay?" Tamar asked.

"After you went upstairs last night," Stanley grinned broadly, "I saw your mother show courage and patience with a dangerous and drunk sailor. To everyone's surprise, she told him that she hoped he would come again, something most of us sincerely hoped he would *not* do."

"And?" Tamar asked.

"And-," Peter replied, "he came early this morning with bags full of fresh celery, carrots, onions, and potatoes."

"Who could have guessed that would happen?" Stanley added.

Tamar beamed with joy. "That's right," she said. "We just never know."

Catholic Worker Personalities

an afterword

Dorothy Day

Dorothy May Day was born on November 8, 1897, in Brooklyn. She worked as a journalist and advocate for peace and justice. She and her common-law husband, Forster Batterham, had one child, Tamar Teresa, born in 1927. After converting to Catholicism, Dorothy broke with Forster and spent time in

Forster Batterham and Dorothy Day on Staten Island in 1925

California, Mexico, and Florida before making her final home in Manhattan. Together with Peter Maurin, Dorothy Day founded the Catholic Worker movement in 1933.

Dorothy Day

A servant of the poor and long-time pacifist, she was the first American to publish a denunciation of nuclear weapons. In the September, 1945, issue of *The Catholic Worker*, she wrote:

> Mr. Truman was jubilant. President Truman. True man; what a strange name, come to think of it. We refer to Jesus Christ as true God and true Man. Truman is a true man of his time in that he was jubilant. He was not a son of God, brother of Christ, brother of the Japanese, jubilating as he did. He went from table to table on the cruiser which was bringing him home from the Big Three conference, telling the great news; "jubilant" the newspapers said. *Jubilate Deo*. We have killed 318,000 Japanese.
>
> That is, we hope we have killed them, the Associated Press, on page one, column one of the *Herald Tribune*, says. The effect is hoped for, not known. It is to be hoped they are vaporized, our Japanese brothers—scattered, men, women, and babies, to the four winds, over the seven seas. Perhaps we will breathe their dust into our nostrils, feel them in the fog of New York on our faces, feel them in the rain on the hills of Easton.
>
> Jubilate Deo. President Truman was jubilant. We have created. We have created destruction. We have created a new element, called Pluto. Nature had nothing to do with it. A cavern below Columbia was the bomb's cradle, born not that men might live but that men might be killed. Brought into being in a cavern and then tried in a desert place in the midst of tempest and lightning, tried out, and then again on

the eve of the Feast of the Transfiguration of our Lord Jesus Christ, on a far-off island in the Eastern Hemisphere, tried out again, this new weapon which conceivably might wipe out mankind, and perhaps the planet itself.

Dropped on a town, one bomb would be equivalent to a severe earthquake and would utterly destroy the place. A scientific brain trust has solved the problem of how to confine and release almost unlimited energy. It is impossible yet to measure its effects.

"We have spent two billion on the greatest scientific gamble in history and won," said President Truman jubilantly.

The papers list the scientists (the murderers) who are credited with perfecting this new weapon. One outstanding authority "who earlier had developed a powerful electrical bombardment machine called the cyclotron, was Professor O. E. Lawrence, a Nobel-prize winner from the University of California. In the heat of the race to unlock the atom, he built the world's most powerful atom-smashing gun, a machine whose electrical projectiles carried charges equivalent to 25,000,000 volts. But such machines were found in the end to be unnecessary. The atom of Uranium-235 was smashed with surprising ease. Science discovered that not sledgehammer blows but subtle taps from slow traveling neutrons managed more on a tuning technique were all that were needed to disintegrate the Uranium-235 atom."

(Remember the tales we used to hear, that one note of a violin, if that note could be discovered, could collapse the Empire State Building. Remember too, that God's voice was heard not in the great and strong wind, not in the earthquake, not in the fire, but "in the whistling of a gentle air.")

Scientists, army officers, great universities (Notre Dame included), and captains of industry-all are given credit lines in the press for their work of preparing the bomb-and other bombs, the president assures us, are in production now.

Great Britain controls the supply of uranium ore in Canada and Rhodesia. We are making the bombs. This new great force will be used for good, the scientists assured us. And then they wiped out a city of 318,000. This was good. The president was jubilant. Today's paper with its columns of description of the new era, The Atomic Era, which this colossal slaughter of the innocents has ushered in, is filled with stories covering every conceivable phase of the new discovery. Pictures of the towns and the industrial plants where the parts are made are spread across the pages. In the forefront of the town of Oak Ridge, Tennessee, is a chapel, a large comfortable-looking chapel benignly settled beside the plant. And the scientists making the first tests in the desert prayed, one newspaper account said.

God, our Creator.

Yes, God is still in the picture. God is not mocked. Today, the day of this so-great news, God made a madman dance and talk who had not spoken for twenty years. God sent a typhoon to damage the carrier *Hornet*. God permitted a fog to obscure vision, and a bomber crashed into the Empire State Building. God permits these things. We have to remember it. We are held in God's hands, all of us, and President Truman, too, and these scientists who have created death but will use it for good. He, God, holds our life and our happiness, our sanity and our health; our lives are in His hands. He is our Creator. Creator.

And as I write, Pigsie, who works in Secaucus, New Jersey, feeding hogs and cleaning out the excrement of the hogs, who comes in once a month to find beauty and surcease and glamour and glory in the drink of the Bowery, trying to drive the hell and the smell out of his nostrils and his life, sleeps on our doorstep, in this best and most advanced and progressive of all possible worlds. And as I write, our cat, Rainbow, slinks by with a shrill rat in her jaws, out of the kitchen closet here at Mott Street. Here in this greatest of cities which covered the cavern where this stupendous discovery was made, which institutes an era of unbelievable richness and power and glory for man.

Everyone says, "I wonder what the Pope thinks of it?" How everyone turns to the Vatican for judgment, even though they do not seem to listen to the voice there! But our Lord himself has already pronounced judgment on the atomic bomb. When James and John (John the beloved) wished to call down fire from heaven on their enemies, Jesus said: "You know not of what spirit you are. The Son of Man came not to destroy souls but to save." He said also, "What you do unto the least of these my brethren, you do unto me."

Dorothy Day died on November 29, 1980, at Maryhouse Catholic Worker in New York City. In 2000, Pope John Paul II declared her "a Servant of God," a first step to canonization. In 2015, during an address to a joint session of the US Congress, Pope Francis described her as one of four "great Americans."

Tamar Teresa Hennessy

Tamar Teresa Hennessy, the only child of the Catholic Worker movement co-founder Dorothy Day, was born on March 4, 1926 in Manhattan. She married William David Hennessy, a farmer and bookseller, at the Catholic Worker farm in Easton, Pennsylvania, in 1944. They had nine children—three sons and six daughters—plus eighteen grandchildren and twelve great-grandchildren. Her husband died

Dorothy reading to Tamar,
about 1933

in 2005. In a 2003 interview by Margot Patterson of *The National Catholic Reporter*, Tamar said of her mother:

> She was traveling a lot, and I was left to be taken care of by various people, and I got very ill. It was hard for both of us. She had her work, and yet at the same time, she had me. She was very devoted. She was torn. She loved her family so much and in so many, many ways she kept me going. I loved the Catholic Worker. It was so exciting. I wouldn't have missed a moment of it.

Tamar's granddaughter, Kate Hennessy, wrote the book *Dorothy Day: The World Will be Saved by Beauty, An Intimate Portrait of My Grandmother*, published in 2016. Her youngest granddaughter, Martha Hennessy, returned to the Catholic Church and has been a member of the Maryhouse Catholic Worker community in New York City's Lower East Side since 2009.

Tamar died at eighty-two on March 25, 2008, in Lebanon, New Hampshire. An obituary appearing in the *Staten Island Advance* observes:

> ... An accomplished spinner and weaver, Ms. Hennessy was also a skilled organic gardener and avid reader. Her great delights were her children and grandchildren, welcoming

Tamar and Dorothy at the Catholic Worker farm,
Easton, Pennsylvania, in 1937

visitors, caring for animals, discussing politics, and listening
to jazz and classical music.

Peter Maurin

Aristide Pierre Maurin was born in Oultet, France, on
May 9, 1877. After a time with the Christian Brothers,
he was drafted into the military. In 1909, he emigrated to
Canada, a country without military conscription. He did
manual labor of many types, traveled widely often by riding
the rails, and taught French lessons. After years of study
and prayer, he embraced voluntary poverty, labor as a gift,
and service to the poor. He favored a movement back to the
land as an antidote for the dehumanization of the Industrial
Revolution. He based his philosophy on the practices of
the early Church. After meeting Dorothy Day in 1932, he
became her inspiration in the Catholic Worker movement.

He communicated many of his ideas in a form that came to be called "Easy Essays" like the one below:

What Makes Us Human

To give and not to take
that is what makes us human.
To serve and not to rule
that is what makes us human.
To help and not to crush
that is what makes us human.
To nourish and not to devour
that is what makes us human.
And if need be
to die and not to live
that is what makes us human.
Ideals and not deals
that is what makes us human.
Creed and not greed
that is what makes us human.

Peter Maurin at Maryhouse, New York City, in 1936

Peter Maurin died at the Catholic Worker farm in Newburgh, New York, on May 15, 1949. His obituary appeared in the *New York Times* and *L'Osservatore Romano*.

From *Time Magazine*:

> Dressed in a castoff suit and consigned to a donated grave, the mortal remains of a poor man were buried last week. These arrangements were appropriate; during most of his life Peter Maurin had slept in no bed of his own and worn no suit that someone had not given away. But to his funeral among the teeming, pushcart-crowded slums of lower Manhattan, Cardinal Spellman himself sent his representative. There were priests representing many Catholic orders, and there were laymen, rich and poor, from places as far away as Chicago. All night long before the funeral, they had come to the rickety storefront where the body lay, to say a prayer or touch their rosaries to the folded hands, for many of them were sure that Peter Maurin was a saint.

Ade Bethune

Ade Bethune was born on January 12, 1914, in Belgium. She emigrated to the US after the first World War. As a nine-

Catholic Worker logos, 1933, left, and 1983, by Ade Bethune

teen-year-old art student, in 1933, she met Dorothy Day who prompted her to begin a career as a Catholic liturgical artist. Her distinctive artwork has appeared countless times in many Catholic Worker newspapers. She died on the sixty-ninth anniversary of the founding of the Catholic Worker movement, May 1, 2002, in Newport, Rhode Island.

book jacket designed by Ade Bethune for Dorothy Day's 1939 book
depicting imaginary view of the back yard of
Saint Joseph's Catholic Worker
115 Mott Street, New York City

*illustrations by Ade Bethune, clockwise from top, left,
include "Homeless," Christ with Little Children," 1935,
and "Saint Telemachus, Peacemaker." Tamar resembled
the child, lower left, in "Christ with Little Children."*

Saint Joseph's Catholic Worker, left, about 1937. Peter Maurin is in top row, hands clasped. Dorothy Day is on second step, eyes closed. Ade Bethune and Tamar are leaning on the rail, left, and detailed, below.

illustrations by Ade Bethune include, from left, Saint Joseph, 1935; Saints Perpetua and Felicitas, and Joy, 1940

A. J. Muste and Dorothy Day at a 1965 draft-card burning

A. J. Muste

Abraham Johannes Muste was born January 8, 1885, in Zierikzee, Netherlands. He and his family emigrated to the United States in 1891. He became a minister in the Dutch Reformed Church in New York City. Influenced by the liberal Social Gospel Movement, he supported the socialist Eugene Victor Debs in 1912. He earned a bachelor of divinity degree from Union Theological Seminary in 1913. A dedicated pacifist, he joined the Fellowship of Reconciliation shortly after its founding in 1916. He later became a Congregational minister and a Quaker. He was active in support of the 1919 women's textile strike in Lawrence, Massachusetts, and became a leader in the American labor movement.

In 1936, he became active in the peace movement and remained an activist throughout World War II. He lectured at Union and Yale Divinity School. He was active in the civil rights movement from its start. In 1951, in order to protest the Cold War, he and forty-eight others filed Thoreau's essay "On the Duty of Civil Disobedience" instead of their tax returns.

He was active in the War Resister's League. He was an early opponent of the Vietnam War. In 1965, he stood on the podium with Dorothy Day as a young Catholic Worker named Tom Cornell and several others burned their draft cards. In a peace effort, Muste traveled to both South Vietnam and North Vietnam. He died February 11, 1967.

Stanley Vishnewski

Stanley Vishnewski was born in 1916. Of the Catholic Worker, he once said, "There's always room for one more, so long as you are not superstitious and don't mind sleeping thirteen in a bed."

Stanley died in 1979. In the December 1979 issue of *The Catholic Worker*, Dorothy Day eulogized him in an article she titled "Knight For A Day." Virtually all of her tribute is reprinted here.

> Stanley was the first Catholic Worker to arrive after my meeting with Peter Maurin. He was a seventeen-year-old Lithuanian from Brooklyn, and it was in the Depression, the early-thirties. His name was really Stanislaus Vish-naukas, but in the Brooklyn school he first went to they found it difficult to pronounce and changed it to Stanley Vishnewski. I personally knew only one of the family, Little Walty, who was much bigger than Stanley. He, or still another brother, worked in a vast steel mill in Baltimore which I visited once. Their father was a tailor and clothed his children well. The first issue of *The Catholic Worker* had come out-a few thousand copies. Stanley's

version of our meeting was that he had met this "little, old lady" (I was in my mid-thirties) carrying a typewriter and with knightly gallantry, had offered to carry my burden. That was the beginning of a long association.

He had, indeed, all but saved my life on two different occasions. The first was during the National Biscuit Company strike when mounted policeman were called out to disperse a mass picket line. I had been distributing leaflets about the right to organize, and Stanley was helping me, when one of the police on a huge horse all but pressed me against a wall. Stanley got between me and the horse and its rider. The second time was when a crazed veteran, who had smuggled food into Biafra, Africa and who went "out of his mind" occasionally, stalked down the long hall at Tivoli,

Stanley Vishnewski, left, selling **The Catholic Worker** *on May 1, 1940 in Union Square, New York City*

passed Stanley's room, and came and threw himself on my bed, burying his face on my shoulder to weep. I could only gasp–"I am not your mother and you are very heavy!" But Stanley was right there in an instant to place a strong hand on his shoulder and say –"The dinner bell just rang." This seemed to bring normalcy to a tense situation, and later the man's friends came after him.

Stanley used to come, these recent years, and have dinner with me every evening, and we watched the television. He loved long walks – especially along Fourth Avenue, where second hand book shops abound. Many a book he found for me to read or re-read.

And then, the sudden announcement – "Stanley is dead!"

Since he, himself, had a bad heart attack some years ago, he was living in Maryhouse, down the hall from my room. He was like an official guest master and delighted in taking new, out-of-town volunteers on walks. He had gone on many a speaking trip these last years, and the little, crippled children at Dorothy Gauchat's Our Lady of the Wayside loved him (as adult audiences did, too). He had a marvelous slide show of the Catholic Worker history over the years. And his famous story, too, about the hungry lion, delighted old and young. I miss Stanley.

Joe Zarella

Joe Zarella was born in 1913. He arrived at Saint Joseph's Catholic Worker in New York City in 1935. In an interview for Rosalie Riegle's book, *Voices of the Catholic Worker*, he said

People would come, and they'd need a bed to sleep. Well, you can't turn somebody away. So you'd get up and give them your bed, and you'd sleep down in the office. For a while there, we were giving our bed away so often, we said,

"To hell with it," you know, and just slept downstairs. If we had some money, we'd give them thirty, thirty-five cents, whatever it was to get a bed in a flophouse.

Julia Porcelli, Dorothy Day, Peter Maurin, and Joe Zarella, from left, in 1940

Ade Bethune, Tamar Forster Hennessy, and Joe Zarella, from left, about 1993

In the lead up to the World War II, he and Dorothy Day went to Washington, DC to make a case for Catholic conscientious objection. During the war, the government jailed four Catholic Workers for opposing military service: Carl Paulson, Hazen Ordway, Jack Thornton, and Joe Czarniecki. Joe Zarella, Gerry Griffin, and Lou Murphy volunteered for American Field Service ambulance units rather than find themselves in the infantry.

Joe had a lifelong admiration for Dorothy Day, whom he always called Miss Day. He went on to become a labor organizer who attended many Catholic Worker gatherings until his death in 2006.

Fritz Eichenberg

Fritz Eichenberg was born on October 24, 1901, to a Jewish family in Cologne, Germany. The destruction of World War I transformed him into a lifelong opponent of war. He studied art in Leipzig and Berlin, where he was an outspoken critic of the Nazis. In 1933, he emigrated to the United States and settled in New York City, where he became a prolific

Fritz Eichenberg

book illustrator. In 1949, he met Dorothy Day at a Quaker conference on religion and publishing. They became friends, and he often donated art that highlighted the

"Christ of the Breadline" by Fritz Eichenberg, 1950,
Art © Estate of Fritz Eichenberg/Licensed by
VAGA, New York, NY

Catholic Worker's work for peace and commitment to serving the poor.

He died in Peace Dale, Rhode Island, on November 30, 1990.

"The Peaceable Kingdom" by Fritz Eichenberg, 1953,
Art © Estate of Fritz Eichenberg/Licensed by
VAGA, New York, NY

"Peter Maurin" by Fritz Eichenberg,
1953, Art © Estate of Fritz Eichenberg/
Licensed by VAGA, New York, NY

Rita Maria Linley Ham Corbin

Rita Maria Linley Ham Corbin was born on May 21, 1930 in Indianapolis, Indiana. She died in Worcester, Massachusetts, on November 17, 2011. In its obituary, *The Brattleboro Reformer* said:

> ... She rebelled against secretarial training and obtained a scholarship to the Franklin School of Professional Art. She also studied at the Art Students' League under printmaker Harold Sternberg and abstract expressionist painter Hans Hoffman, but she said her best education came from visiting art museums and galleries, exploring the city, and drawing the ordinary people she saw. In 1950, she became involved in the Catholic Worker movement. The founder, Dorothy Day, with whom she became

"Jesus Crucified Again, top, and "No More War Refugees," posters Rita made for Saints Francis and Thérèse Catholic Worker demonstrations

close friends, immediately set Rita to work illustrating *The Catholic Worker* newspaper. Rita became a lifelong contributor as one of three primary Catholic Worker artists, along with Fritz Eichenberg and Ade Bethune. In 1954, she

two Christmas cards by Rita Corbin

married Martin Joseph Corbin, editor and literary critic. They worked on *Liberation* magazine with activist Dave Dellinger ...

When an interviewer once asked her, 'Do you believe the artist has a social responsibility?" She responded, "Everyone has a social responsibility."

For several years in the 1990s, Rita lived in Worcester, with Tom Lewis, a longtime artist and activist. During that time, she created numerous original works for the pages of the Saints Francis & Thérèse Catholic Worker community's newspaper, *The Catholic Radical.* She also made posters and banners for Catholic Worker demonstrations.

Brian Kavanagh

Brian Kavanagh was born on September 8, 1943 in Meriden, Connecticut. After earning a BA from the University of Hartford Art School, he became an art teacher. In the 1980s, he involved himself increasingly in the peace movement. In 1993, shortly after the Hartford Catholic Worker opened its doors, he became a member and has lived there ever since. Brian donates his work to Catholic Worker communities.

*Brian Kavanagh's "On the Other End," left, and
"Masters of War"*

*Brian Kavanagh's "Guantanamo Christ," top, from a banner made
at the request of Jackie Allen-Douçot of the
Hartford Catholic Worker for the 2007 Witness Against Torture
march in Cuba calling for the release of detainees held at
Guantanamo by the US military and
Kavanagh's "Just War Theory"*

Bibliography

Coles, Robert. *Dorothy Day: A Radical Devotion*. Addison-Wesley Publishing. Reading, Massachusetts, 1987.

Day, Dorothy. *The Long Loneliness*. Harper and Row Publishers. New York, New York, 1952.

Ellis, Marc H. *Peter Maurin: Prophet in the Twentieth Century*. Paulist Press. Ramsey, New Jersey, 1981.

Hennessy, Kate. *Dorothy Day: The World Will Be Saved by Beauty: An Intimate Portrait of My Grandmother*. Scribner, an imprint of Simon and Schuster. New York, New York, 2017.

Piehl, Mel. *Breaking Bread: The Catholic Worker And the Origin of Catholic Radicalism in America*. Temple, University Press. Philadelphia, 1982.

About the Author

Scott Schaeffer-Duffy and his wife, Claire, have been Catholic Workers since 1982. They are the parents of four children and grandparents of three. Scott is the author of *Nothing Is Impossible: stories from the life of a Catholic Worker*, 2016, Haley's.

Scott welcomes reader questions and comments. He is available for talks, readings, and signings.

Readers can contact him as follows:

Scott Schaeffer-Duffy

Saints Francis & Thérèse Catholic Worker

52 Mason Street

Worcester, MA 01610 USA

theresecw2@gmail.com

*Author Scott Schaeffer-Duffy with his grandchildren,
from left, Theo, Frances, and May.*

Colophon

Text for *Murder on Mott Street* is set in Adobe Caslon
Pro. Caslon is the name given to serif typefaces designed by
William Caslon I (c. 1692–1766) in London or inspired by
his work.

Caslon worked as an engraver of punches, the masters
used to stamp the moulds or matrices used to cast metal type.
He worked in the tradition of what is now called old-style
serif letter design,that produced letters with a relatively
organic structure resembling handwriting with a pen. Caslon
established a tradition of engraving type in London, which
previously had not been common. His typefaces established
a strong reputation for their quality and their attractive
appearance, suitable for extended passages of text.

Caslon's typefaces were popular in his lifetime and beyond,
and after a brief period of eclipse in the early nineteenth
century, they returned to popularity, particularly for setting
printed body text and books. Many revivals exist, with varying
faithfulness to Caslon's original design. Modern Caslon
revivals also often add features such as a matching boldface.

Titles for *Murder on Mott Street* are sent in Bodoni, the name given to the serif typefaces first designed by Giambattista Bodoni (1740–1813) in the late eighteenth century and frequently revived since.Bodoni's typefaces are classified as didone or modern. Bodoni followed the ideas of John Baskerville, as found in the printing type Baskerville but he took them to a more extreme conclusion.

Bodoni had a long career, and his designs changed and varied, ending with a typeface of a slightly condensed underlying structure.

When first released, Bodoni and other didone fonts were called classical designs because of their rational structure. They came to be called modern serif fonts and then, until the mid twentieth century, they were known as didone designs. Bodoni's later designs are rightfully called modern, but the earlier designs are now called transitional.